The Royal Gordanos
A Royal's Touch
A Royal's Pursuit
Craving a Royal

The Lucifer Brothers
The Devil is my Boss

I0542411

The Lucifer Brothers

THE DEVIL IS MY BOSS

MAKAYLA ROBERTS

The Devil is my Boss
ISBN # 978-1-83943-858-5
©Copyright Makayla Roberts 2020
Cover Art by Erin Dameron-Hill ©Copyright March 2020
Interior text design by Claire Siemaszkiewicz
Totally Bound Publishing

Published in 2020 by Totally Bound Publishing, United Kingdom.

Totally Bound Publishing is an imprint of Totally Entwined Group Limited.

THE DEVIL IS MY BOSS

Chapter One

"I quit!"

The shout was followed by the furious slamming of a file cabinet. Rhys Lucifer stood near the door, the only exit in the spacious office. Well, not unless one counted the floor-to-ceiling windows, though he doubted his employee was mad enough to jump to his death. "Come now, Ivan. We can talk about this."

The male whirled around, narrowing his eyes in disbelief. "Talk? There's nothing to talk about!" He slammed another drawer then used one arm to sweep his personal belongings off his desk and into the cardboard box he held under his other arm. "Seven months of utter hell."

"Well, we are in Sheol," Rhys drawled, not at all helping the situation, "which is technically what's referred to as —"

"I know where the fuck we are," Ivan snarled. He pointed a shaking finger at Rhys, his Russian accent thick with his madness. "This job is… It's… I don't even have the words for it, but I quit! No demon in their right mind should ever agree to this position. I don't know what I was thinking."

Money, no doubt. Money and power, Rhys thought. It was the same with everyone who was brave enough to take on the job as his COO.

Rhys grunted and shifted his weight to one leg as he watched his chief operating officer march around the mahogany desk to stalk across the room, his box tucked a bit too tightly under one arm. His eyes were desolate with dark circles that spoke of restless nights, the uncombed toupée atop his head lopsided. There was a shadow across his jaw, making it clear that he hadn't shaved in several days, either.

"I'll admit it's a...difficult position, but—"

"Difficult?" Ivan echoed on a bark of laughter. "I've had less than fifteen hours of sleep in the past week." He waved his free arm to indicate the piles upon piles of paper stacked on the floor. The movement caused his toupée to slip from his head and fall onto the desk, not that he seemed to notice. "All this work is far too much for one person to do, and between the board meetings, employee requests and upcoming events—never mind that with the wars going on topside, the mortal death tolls increase each day. No way, man. I quit! I'm done."

Rhys shifted his weight to his other leg, mild panic welling at the notion that the employee he needed the most to help him through these critical times was quitting on him. *Again.* "Ivan, please. Think about what you're doing. What about the Séance Convention coming up? I can't go it alone, and you're the only one with the proper knowledge to accompany me. Plus, there's no time to train anyone to fill your position before then." He paused. "I'll give you a bonus. How does an extra four thousand sen sound?"

Slowly, Ivan turned to face Rhys. His irises changed from black to red, a sure sign of a pissed-off demon. It didn't matter that Rhys was his boss or that he was the oldest son of one of the most important men in the underworld—nor did it seem to matter that, at six-three, Rhys had a good foot and a half on him. The look he was receiving was one of pure disgust.

In fluent Russian, Ivan jabbed a finger in the center of Rhys' chest and said, "Fuck that convention, and you can shove your money up your ass."

He snatched his toupée off the desk and slammed it on top of his head. Then he marched out of the office.

Chin dropping to his chest, Rhys watched Ivan storm down the maze of cubicles lining the floor and to the far side, where a bank of elevators sat behind a set of glass doors. His now-former employee tapped his foot as he waited for one of the elevators to arrive. When it did, he stepped inside and faced Rhys and the multiple pairs of eyes watching him. Then, just as the doors slid closed, he raised his hand high and gave them all the bird.

And that was it. Ivan was gone, having quit after only seven months. Rhys shouldn't have been shocked, since the man before Ivan had resigned after an even shorter time. *Hell's bells.* He'd taken over this portion of the family company twenty years ago and, in that time, he'd lost double the number of COOs. Not that any of them had been particularly good at their job, but *someone* needed to fill the position, and the majority of them had all the qualifications.

Now he was back at square one, with large shoes to fill and less than two weeks to do so. *Just freaking terrific.*

With a dull throb forming between his brows, he exited the office and closed the door. When he glanced at his employees watching him with wide eyes, he

9

snapped, "Get back to work!" There was an immediate clack of keyboards as everyone did as commanded, no doubt fearing he was in a firing type of mood.

He relaxed his expression to one of ice, striding across the floor to the elevators. Gods below, he needed a damn drink. No, he needed the whole bottle and then some. It'd been a long-ass day, and it wasn't even eight o'clock yet, damn it all.

Stepping onto the elevator, he pressed the arrow going up with far more force than needed. The ride up was four floors, but it may as well have been the entire thirty-plus that made up this wing of the building. When the doors opened once more, he stormed out, heading for his private office.

He rounded a corner and his secretary perked up. "Good morning, Rhys…" She trailed off, her smile waning as she took in his fuming expression.

His steps never faltered as he strode past her. "Pull up a list of this division's employees and compile a separate list of those qualified to take Ivan's place."

Kelle's eyes widened a bit. "Yes, sir," she responded, swiveling in her chair to face her computer. There was no hesitation, no questions asked, just swift obedience, which was one of the reasons Rhys had hired her a decade before. He was a man who gave orders and expected them to be carried out to the fullest. Otherwise, someone ended up demoted – or fired.

And that was just him being polite.

With a deep sigh, Rhys entered his office. He skipped his desk and opted for the black leather sofa across the room.

Ten days. He had ten days to dig through his employees to determine which one would be qualified enough to take on the job of COO. Granted, it was a tough spot, but the benefits that came with it were incredible compared to positions of lower status. Anyone should feel honored to be promoted, especially in this line of work.

As his mind began to wander, there was a sharp knock at the door. The trespasser didn't wait for a response, proceeding to open the door. With another deep sigh, Rhys didn't bother sitting up. There was no point. He already knew who it was. With his heightened senses, the familiar scent of eucalyptus and antibacterial hand sanitizer was always a dead giveaway that his younger brother, Quin, was nearby. The man was a germaphobe. It would have been laughable, given his large six-six frame, but the sad truth behind it was one only the three brothers knew.

And, of course, the smell of dark cinnamon spices soon followed, signaling the entrance of his even younger brother, Thorne. They were the only two beings at Elysium Underworld Corp who possessed the balls to intrude on his privacy without permission.

One of them let out a low whistle as they made themselves comfortable in the matching leather armchairs around him. "Looks like the rumors are true," Quin commented, a touch of humor in his deep voice. "Your officer walked out on you again."

Rhys grunted, squeezing his eyes shut in frustration. "At the most inconvenient of times," he growled, annoyed with the entire situation. And, from past experiences, he was about to become even more so. His brothers usually came to enjoy watching him soak in misery, torturing him with their ill-conceived jokes.

"Any idea who you're going to get to replace him?" Thorne asked, though his tone suggested he couldn't give two shits.

"Not a clue," Rhys retorted. He didn't know a quarter of his employees, truth be told. There was no point in making much effort when people were always coming and going. The handful he did know were the important ones he had to deal with throughout the week, like Kelle and Ivan.

"It sucks, brother. I feel for you."

Rhys flipped his brother off, eliciting a dark chuckle. "If you two aren't going to offer any help, you can just get the fuck out."

"Hey, there's no need to be rude," Quin drawled. "We actually *did* come to help. I did, anyway. Thorne is here to be his usual self."

"Damn right," Thorne crooned.

Rhys shook his head and straightened to peer at his brothers. Though the three couldn't be more different personality-wise, the similarities in appearance made it clear that they were related. All three of them had the same dark brown hair. Unlike Rhys, who kept a short clean cut, Quin's was a bit longer, the ends curling just under his chin. Thorne, however, wore his to his shoulders, several of the thick strands shot through with natural blond highlights from prolonged exposure to the sun topside. All three had brown eyes, though Quin's were lighter in color, more along the lines of toffee, and Thorne had golden flecks around the pupils. Rhys' jawline was more defined, but Quin's lips were fuller and Thorne's nose was crooked, after having been broken one too many times.

And though they each had two six-inch-tall, curved horns rising from the tops of their heads, the spiraling patterns engraved on them were similar, but not the same, having appeared after they'd reached maturity.

"How the hell do you two know that Ivan quit?" Rhys demanded. "It hasn't even been a full twenty minutes since he walked out."

"Oh, you know," Thorne responded, throwing one leg over the arm of his chair. "Word travels fast around here. Rumors spread like wildfire among the office geeks."

Quin snorted. "For sure. Plus, someone uploaded a video of the whole thing on Fangsbook. It's already gotten a thousand views."

That much was true. Not about the video, but the other bit. Though every day was busy for his employees, they still made time to babble and converse. Secrets never lasted very long. "So, you two merrily shirked your duties to help me find a replacement?"

Quin shrugged, the thick muscles making up his shoulders rippling under his button-up shirt. His usual attire wasn't a full business suit like Rhys preferred. His brother always wore slacks, khakis or dress pants with either a polo or a button shirt tucked at the waist. Thorne, on the other hand, didn't even try. As the head of the field workers division, he spent a lot of time topside and was always active, so there was no need for him to dress as professionally as Rhys and Quin did. Still, Rhys had encouraged him several times over the decades to do so, to set an example for his own employees.

He'd ignored him, of course. As the youngest, Thorne had always been something of a wild child, the typical rebellious bad boy who broke all the rules and did what he wanted. Sitting across from Rhys, he was dressed in ripped jeans and a black T-shirt with some rock band logo on it. *Yeah, real fucking professional.*

"Pretty much," Quin answered, leaning back in his chair. He formed a triangle with his hands, drumming his fingers against each other in thought. "Between the three of us, it shouldn't take more than an hour to scan through your workers. We'll start with the higher-ranked ones then move on to the lower levels. We can separate them into two piles—the maybes and the rejects."

Rhys snorted. "You make it sound as though they're nothing more than test subjects."

Quin shrugged. "In a way, they are. You've had four COOs quit in the last five years, and the numbers beyond that are even more pitiful. It's a tough position, so you need someone with a stiff backbone. And no offense, but most of your people are—"

"Weak," Thorne suggested.

"That's a polite way of putting it."

Rhys rolled his eyes and stood. "They may think the job is overwhelming, but it can't even lift a candle to the shit I have to deal with."

"True," Quin and Thorne said in unison.

Rhys ambled out of his office, rounding a corner to approach Kelle. She was focused on her computer monitor. Without looking at him, she said, "I've filtered out anyone with excessive absences or tardiness, anyone who's worked here for less than five years and anyone with complaints, suspensions, demotions or write-ups against them."

Rhys gave a curt nod. "Excellent. How many does that leave us with?"

She glanced up at him with sympathy. "It didn't even cut the list in half. There's two thousand, nine hundred and thirty-nine left."

Rhys' tiny flare of relief was squashed. No wonder she'd moved so fast. There was hardly any trimming she'd had to do. "Terrific," he grouched. "Reschedule any meetings this morning to after lunch. Then divide the list into three sections, one each for Quinton, Thorne and me."

Kelle nodded. "Yes, sir."

He returned to his office, reclaiming his seat on the couch. "The list has been narrowed down to a little less than three thousand. You might as well get comfortable, boys."

Both grunted, but he knew they truly didn't mind helping, no matter how much they enjoyed mocking him. They knew the stress that came with his job.

There were four main regions in Sheol—otherwise known as the underworld located beneath the earth—and each was ruled by a major family name that had been around since its birth. Elysium Underworld Corporation was a business in the Elysium region, of course. Rhys, Quinton and Thorne were all Lucifers, the three sons born from Damien Lucifer. As a way to better organize the constant arrival and departure of mortal souls, a thousand years ago Damien and two other family leaders had built massive corporate-style buildings in their separate regions to better control and keep track of the souls sent there.

Similar to the other three regions, entire cities had been built around EUC, which had influenced the creation of similar formations topside. That was right. As much as the humans believed that they'd thought of everything, the very world they knew had been taught to them by demons long ago, and only a select few mortals were aware of the truth.

After coming of age, Rhys had taken over EUC when his father had retired. As his brothers had gained the knowledge to join him in management, the business was then divided into three main sections to ease his workload—the Fielders, the Processing Center and the Soul Distribution Center.

Thorne was CEO of the first. The Field workers included reapers and charons. The reapers—aka angels of death—were assigned to mortals who were on the verge of dying, whether from illness, failing health or even the unexpected piano falling from the sky. They gathered the souls of dead mortals topside and brought them to the charons. Similar to Charon in Greek mythology, charons were the demons who walked between the human and demon world, delivering souls to EUC.

That would place them in the Processing Center, which was controlled by Quin. There, the souls were detained in a vast holding cell and processed for paperwork. The admin took down every bit of information about the soul, collecting every thought and action from the moment they had been born up until their death. Once the paperwork was complete, it was sent to the Soul Distribution Center, which was Rhys' division.

Charged with uploading the paperwork into specialized databases designed to keep track of every soul born and reborn, it was the SDC's job to make sure the information taken from each soul's past life was properly formatted. Finally, at the end of each day, all the paperwork was to be typed into a report that went through one final stop for organizing, to make sure each soul was dispersed correctly.

One of three things happened to a soul after that. If a mortal died before its time, it would be given a second chance at life, in which case charons would carry the soul back to the reapers to return to their human bodies before the corpse became damaged. The other two options determined if the soul could be reborn or would be destroyed.

Very rarely did the latter happen. When a soul was to be reborn, the COO looked over each one and decided where to distribute it. For those who had lived a life over-indulging in one of the seven deadly sins, they would be faced with some sort of punishment, needing to work for several months or years to earn their freedom to be reborn again. From there, the soul would be confined and transported to Asphodel to receive its sentence. The souls who had led good, meaningful lives were at the top of the list to be reborn into another mortal form, so would be sent off to The Meadows. Or, as Thorne called it, 'Hippie Land', for the serene atmosphere that gave souls the impression of being in 'heaven'.

Still, it was up to Rhys' COO to go through the thousands upon thousands of souls on the paperwork sent in weekly to make the decision on each soul, as well as assist in overlooking the rest of the division to make sure everything ran with ease.

Yeah, they were *very* large shoes to fill, and since Rhys had more than enough of his own problems to deal with, he didn't have the time to begin sorting through the paperwork himself. Free time just didn't exist in his life anymore.

A knock sounded, making Rhys blink to the present. "Enter," he commanded.

Kelle strolled in, her short legs clad in bright pink nylons, crossed the distance to where all three brothers sat. "Here are your lists, sir. I've organized them according to who has worked here the longest."

Thorne whistled in appreciation. "Impressive," he complimented, surveying Kelle's small frame in a way that indicated he wasn't just talking about her work.

Kelle narrowed her dark eyes, giving a toss of her hair to make the bite mark on the side of her neck evident. It was a symbol of her mating, making her off-limits to any other demon. Kelle was a wolf shifter. Like most other demons, wolves mated for life, and they were damn territorial. Not that it would stop Thorne from hitting on one of them, but Kelle was devoted to her mate.

Thorne grinned, wiggling his eyebrows at her. "I can bite just as hard as your mate, Kelle."

She rolled her eyes, turning her back to stroll away. "Even if I wasn't mated, that's a big fat 'hell no'."

"Fifty refusals eventually turns into a yes," Thorne called after her.

Just before exiting, Kelle turned to flash red eyes at him. "Given that you've fucked half your employees and just as many in our and Quin's divisions, I repeat. Hell. *No*." With that, she slammed the door behind herself, her heels clapping against the marble flooring as she stormed away.

Rhys shook his head. Thorne had once broken the heart of one of Kelle's friends. He could have been forgiven had he shown remorse, but, of course, such an emotion always seemed to elude him. Thorne was even less fond of emotional attachments than Rhys, though, unlike him, his brother was a dick about it.

Thorne chuckled, turning back to his brothers with a wide grin. "She totally wants me."

Quin shook his head in dismay. "You and I must have different definitions for the word 'want', brother. The look she gave was pure venom."

Thorne shrugged. "She'll come around. They always do."

Rhys waved aside their banter. "Let's get to work, if you two are done."

Both brothers shifted to focus on the stacks of paper before them. For several moments, the three of them just stared and stared…then stared some more. Three men. Three five-inch-high piles to sort through.

What. A. Drag.

Chapter Two

Remi glanced at the sterling silver watch strapped around her wrist and grimaced. Eight-o-five in the morning. She wasn't just late for work. She was late as *hell*. Pun intended.

What was this, her third tardy since last week? Yeah, Ivan was going to kill her. Every employee at the office could be late, pull no-call-no-shows or just walk out before their shift was over with no explanation and the pudgy troll wouldn't bat an eye. But if Remi hit the clock thirty seconds too late, he would go into a screaming rage.

Yet when she glanced at her cell phone, she was surprised she didn't have any missed calls from her boss. There wasn't a single voicemail or text message, despite her being an hour and five…no, an hour and six minutes late. If she were lucky, he'd be at one of his board meetings and hadn't noticed her missing.

Ah, hell. It wasn't like it could have been helped. She'd seen the *cutest* hellhound puppy on the way to work and had to pet it. Petting the stray pup had turned into her picking it up and detouring to the closest pet store, where she'd spent two hundred sen on supplies. Of course, she couldn't bring the supplies or the puppy to work, so she'd had to go back home, unload her bags and set up the spare room with a bowl of water, puppy chow, a doggy bed three times the size of the dog and several toys, making the little hound as comfortable as demonly possible.

It was only after all that time that she'd remembered she'd better get a move on before Ivan went into another one of his explosive temper tantrums over her tardiness.

Jeez, what is his problem with me, anyway? Sure, she was late every now and then—okay, more often than not—but she couldn't help it. Things just happened to pop up at the most inopportune times. In this case, it was a tiny black-and-white hellhound puppy she'd named Pepper who'd needed her. Who knew what would have happened if she'd left the sweet baby out there all alone? She'd saved Pepper's life! Surely that constituted a good reason to be late.

Yeah, like Ivan would fall for that BS. He was a real stickler for the rules, and his panties had been growing tighter each passing month. Sooner or later the man was going to snap.

He had the worst job at EUC, after all. Having to go through mountains of paperwork and determine the correct fate of each soul that came through their workplace? Yeah, that was no fun. And if that wasn't bad enough, it was no secret that if the COO misjudged a soul, there would be absolute hell to pay. Getting fired from such a high position was the least of the COO's worries, should he make such a crucial mistake.

Remi snorted. *It sucks to be you, Ivan*, she thought, as she crossed the street to the massive building that was

Elysium Underworld Corp. Far larger than most structures built by the humans topside, EUC took up a mile in all directions, stretching far and wide to encompass the space needed for the number of employees and souls wandering in and out daily. If the expanse of land wasn't enough to gawk at, EUC rose high into the permanent night sky as a towering building that wasn't the tallest in the city, but it was the widest.

Remi sauntered through the revolving doors to the front lobby. The heels of her black pumps *tap, tap, tap*ped with each step on the black-and-gold marble flooring. It was mid-spring topside in the US above them, which meant the weather was just as lovely down here in Elysium-Sheol, despite the fact that there was never a shred of sunlight. She'd dressed for the warmth in a knee-length pencil skirt with a pretty floral blouse. Ivan would scold her and say she was dressed too casually, but they both knew it was a lie. Compared to the way most of the women dressed in the other two wings of EUC, she could have passed for a nun. The troll just wanted something to complain about.

After making her way to the large bank of elevators, she waited for one to arrive. She didn't mind being late. Every one of her peers knew she was a good worker, often finishing hours before them. No one complained, because instead of lounging around riding the clock, she helped everyone else finish their tasks to prevent their division from getting backed up. There had even been a few occasions when Ivan had enlisted her help in finishing *his* paperwork.

She snorted at the understatement. Well, more than a 'few' occasions. And she didn't 'help' him with his work. She *did* it for him while *he* lazed around, wasting the day away. For the past month and a half, he'd spent maybe the last three days doing his job, while she did everything the rest of the time. In return, she'd never gotten a simple 'thank you'. He didn't even give her passes on being late. He was an asswipe through and through.

The elevator *dinged* and she stepped on. At first glance, the panel of buttons that took up an entire wall was complex and resembled something out of a futuristic sci-fi movie, but, after using it for three years, she was accustomed to working the system.

Unlike ordinary elevators that went up and down, the ones at EUC went sideways as well, making maneuvering through the different wings much easier. Remi pressed the same three buttons she used on a daily basis, humming to herself as the ride carried her to the Soul Distribution Center. She pulled out her phone and scrolled through her newsfeed on Fangsbook, one of the social networking apps for demons in Sheol. Nothing new or exciting, except...

She brought her phone closer to her face, rereading the status posted by one of her coworkers, along with an attached video. "Ivan quit?" she asked aloud. "No way." She tapped on the video, watching with wide eyes as Ivan lost his marbles, snapping and snarling and sending papers flying as he stormed around. The video ended with him flipping everyone off and disappearing into the elevator.

Remi replayed the video, throwing her head back and laughing with glee. "Thank you, Hades," she chuckled, pleased to have avoided another tongue lashing. She closed the app and slid the cell into her purse as the elevator slowed to a stop. It had been expected, hadn't it? Since the day she'd been hired, there had been three different chief operating officers coming and going, unable to maintain the position for long before falling off the deep end. However, she'd never seen any of them throw a tantrum as bad as the one Ivan had just done. *Bummer.* She wondered what had pushed him over the edge.

The doors opened and Remi exited, relaxing her shoulders as she was able to breathe without looking over her shoulder for her boss.

Rounding a corner, she smiled at the two receptionists sitting behind the desks outside a door leading to the large room of cubicles. "Good morning, ladies," she greeted them. They were both on the phone, but they paused to greet her in return. Remi carried on to the door beyond.

Even if she hadn't watched the video on Fangsbook, she would have known something was up with the tension in the air, so thick it was damn near tangible. She scanned what looked like a mini tornado had whirled through. *Never let it be said Ivan wasn't a total drama queen.* If he was going down, he was going to throw a big scene to leave his mark behind.

Remi sighed as she approached her cubicle. She sank into the chair, reaching to start her computer. There were several thick folders already stacked on her desk, along with a handful of sticky notes with requests and reminders on them. She didn't fret, though. The extra paperwork only made her crack her knuckles in anticipation. She loved the challenge of her job.

The Soul Distribution Center was like an ant colony. Everyone on their floor had an important job to do, and that was to make sure the data from the papers was keyed into their database. It was easy, but it was time-consuming, which was why a lot of people asked to work in the other two divisions when applying for a job.

Remi hadn't cared which place she was hired into. She'd just wanted to move to the infamous underworld city and find her own way. It was either that or remain hidden in the shadows while her parents set her up to marry some stranger who could take over their business. Her parents were stuck on the 'men work while the women sit pretty' mindset. It didn't matter that she'd proven she was capable of running the business herself or that she'd earned several business degrees in the human schools topside for that reason alone. They were persistent in thinking she needed a man to take care of her.

Blech… No freaking thanks. Her younger sister might be all for the idea of letting a man pamper her while she didn't have to lift a finger, but not Remi. She believed in working for her own benefit, and she'd managed just fine for the past decade, more so since she'd moved to Sheol five years before.

Two years after that, when she'd heard about the job openings for Elysium Underworld Corp, she'd wasted no time in applying for the first thing she'd seen, which was a clerk. She'd been interviewed, hired the next day and hadn't regretted a moment since then.

She loved her job. She loved her coworkers. She loved the peace of being able to provide for herself. Furthermore, she loved being free — free to do what she wanted, free to date who she wanted, free to just be…free. She'd found something she was good at, and she loved it.

It was far more than what awaited her back home. A life of hiding from her true heritage, pretending to be a human when the truth of her blood was so much deeper, was not a way to live, especially not when she had parents whose only concern was for themselves and their lavish lifestyle. Her father's last words to her still rang through her mind. *'You are no longer welcome here until you've decided to give up on this ridiculous independence of yours.'*

While she couldn't give two shits about her parents abandoning her, she missed her younger sister something fierce. She loved her new life, but since she'd refused to tell anyone who and what she was, it made getting close to people rather difficult.

"Oh, my gods, Remi. You missed all the action," a voice called, dragging out the S sound in his words like a snake.

Remi glanced up at her cube neighbor, Silas, the ping of loneliness disappearing to the back of her mind. *The very definition of flamboyant…* It didn't bother her in the least bit that the male's natural green hair was styled in a flippy, young Justin Bieber way or that the heavy glittery makeup on his slanted eyes made him look like some kind of glitzy K-pop star. Nor did she bat an eye at his slender build dressed in a bubblegum pink button-up shirt with cotton candy-blue capri pants and matching glittery shoes. After three years of working beside him, she was used to his flashy fashion choices.

If he liked it, she loved it.

Besides, the plain beige walls and drab gray carpet of their floor could always use a splash of color.

Remi held her phone in her hand, shaking the blank screen at him. "I saw the video." She pouted. "But I wish I could've seen it in person. I would have had the popcorn ready."

"Seconded," a female said, joining them. Gracie, whose cubicle was on the other side of Remi's, popped her head over the wall separating them. She was another good friend, and the name fit her — image-wise, at least. She had a halo of golden curls brushing her shoulders and large baby-blue eyes giving her an innocent appearance. However, with a sharp tongue that could lash a hardened warrior to pieces, she was all demon at heart.

Remi blinked at her in surprise. "Gracie, you missed the show, too?"

Gracie let out a soft sigh, annoyance crossing her pretty features. Even her voice was light and lilting. "Unfortunately, I missed the whole thing. Somebody left their man-purse in the car and *desperately* needed it here with him." At that, she narrowed her eyes at Silas.

He placed a hand to his chest, offended. "Oh, *puh-lease*! It's a fanny pack, not a purse, and it had my inhaler in it. It's a very long walk from here to the parking garage. I could have had an asthma attack before I made it halfway. Asthma attacks can lead to death, you know."

Gracie rolled her eyes. "You're such a drama queen. Demons don't get asthma attacks, fool. That's a human condition. We all know your inhaler is infused with alco—"

"Sh-h-h!" Silas whispered, glancing around in suspicion. He lowered his voice. "Are you trying to get me in trouble? Don't go saying such things out loud."

Remi sighed, leaning into the mesh back of her chair. "I haven't been here ten minutes, and you two are giving me a migraine."

Silas grinned, the patches of iridescent scales around his eyes shimmering in the overhead light. "What else is new?"

She shook her head, facing her computer. While she scanned through her emails, she asked, "Did something happen to make Ivan snap or was he already pissed when he came in?"

"Lucille says he was looking for you when he came in, but he seemed fine at first," Gracie answered. "Well, as fine as Ivan can ever be."

Remi rolled her eyes. "Of course he was looking for me, no doubt to chew me out about the gods know what. I swear… If it isn't one thing, it's another."

Silas snorted. "I'll say. The man totally had it out for you."

"Yeah," Gracie agreed, a sly smile curling her lips. "It's only because you can do his job ten times better than him, and if the big man upstairs found out, he'd lose all his benefits."

Remi snorted, waving that aside. Done checking the email reminders, she went through her files to pull up the spreadsheet system they used to enter data from the mortal souls' paperwork. "He didn't have anything to worry about. I wouldn't take his position, even if it was offered to me on a silver platter."

Gracie tilted her head to the side, her curls bouncing with the movement. "You should go for it, Rem. Everyone here already turns to you instead of Ivan. And every time there's some kind of crisis, you're the one to fix it."

"Yeah," Silas chimed in. "Not to mention that people trust you, and you know how to lead without being a total bitch. I say you should turn your resume into Mr. Lucifer."

Remi snorted again, shaking her head in denial. "As tempting as that sounds, it's a 'no' from me," she drawled. "I'm comfortable where I'm at. I can be a data clerk and still assist everyone else. Besides, there are plenty of other people higher than me who are better qualified for that spot."

All three friends looked at one another. After a moment of silence, they laughed aloud. "Yeah, right," Silas said on a chuckle.

"Speaking of Mr. Lucifer," Gracie said, a star-struck look settling on her features. "I heard he made an appearance to speak to Ivan. I would have given a lung and a limb just to see him."

Silas leaned forward, placing his chin on his folded arms. His eyes took on a dreamy stare. "You and me both, Grace. That's one man I would not mind sinking my fangs into." To emphasize his point, he flicked his forked tongue over the short, yet sharp tips of his incisors.

Remi lifted an eyebrow. "I've never met him, but from what I hear, he and his brothers are hetero, Silas."

Silas arched a brow of his own. "Give me five minutes alone with one of them and they won't be."

The two women chuckled at that. Remi turned to the pile of folders on her desk. She cracked her knuckles. "If you guys don't mind, I need to get started on these before I have to stay overnight."

Gracie scoffed. "You and I know good and well that you'll be three-quarters of the way finished before lunchtime." Even as she said it, she pushed off the wall and Remi heard the creak of a chair as Gracie flopped down.

Silas did the same. "The one with the least amount of work done by lunch has to pay."

"Deal," Remi said. She opened the first folder, scanning over the stapled papers of her first soul of the day. Without glancing at her computer screen, she began transferring the information from the papers into the data system.

With Ivan gone, she was glad to catch a break from having him on her case. She did, however, wonder who his replacement would be. COO of the Soul Distribution Center was the toughest job to have, just under the CEO's status. One slip could end in termination. And she didn't mean just being fired.

Though Sheol was home to ninety-five percent of the demon population, the remaining five lived either topside or in Tartarus, the realm below Sheol. Solely ruled by Hades — aka Orcus aka Pluto and a hundred other names made up by the varying human religions — the god was strict over mortal souls being distributed to the correct destination. If there was even the slightest of slipups, both the COO and the CEO would have to answer to him, if the incident couldn't be fixed in time. And while it was no secret that Hades favored the Lucifers over the other three major families — the Belials, the Leviathans and the Dagons — the ruthless god wasn't merciful toward anyone.

With a grimace, Remi focused on the work at hand. Her heart went out to the unlucky bastard who would have to take Ivan's spot.

Chapter Three

"There. That's the last of them," Rhys said on a sigh. Contrary to their previous assumption, it had taken the brothers four and a half hours to finish digging through the piles, only to come up with fifteen 'maybe' candidates. The sad part was, the only thing strong about them was the 'maybe', because their records were quite pitiful. Furthermore, not a single one of them had the slightest clue how to do Ivan's job.

Not even his employees in the upper ranks were qualified for the position, which added to Rhys' sour mood. It went to show how incompetent his people were. After the convention, he'd be sure to return order to them. Perhaps they'd gotten too comfortable with his lingering absences or the managers overseeing them were doing a piss-poor job, but he would correct that as soon as possible.

"So, we're done here?" Thorne asked, tilting his head left and right to crack his neck. Rhys winced. He hated when his brother did that.

"*You're* done," Rhys said, standing. He gathered the pile of maybes, shaking his head in annoyance. "I'm going to get Kelle to assemble these candidates so I can interview them. A bunch of sorry asses, but one of them is bound to not be a complete failure."

Quin grunted as he rose, as well. He brought out his trusty tube of sanitizer and squeezed a pea-sized amount into his palm. "Careful not to tempt fate, brother. It's like how in the movies when someone says, *'What's the worst that could happen?'* Then disaster befalls them."

Rhys blinked in confusion. "What the devil are you talking about?"

Thorne gave a rueful shake of his head. "You really need to get out more, Rhys, if you don't even know what that cliché is. That stick is sliding farther and farther up your ass."

Rhys scowled. "Piss off." He whirled around then crossed the carpet toward the door. He was a busy man. He didn't have time to kick back and keep up with the latest Trollywood entertainment bullshit. He opened the door and approached Kelle's desk. When she peered at him, he handed her the papers. "Email these people and have them scheduled for an interview — the sooner the better."

Kelle nodded. "Very well." When he started to turn away, Kelle's phone rang. She answered it right away. After listening for several moments, she sucked in a sharp breath. "Okay, I'll notify him. Thanks."

Rhys tensed. He threw his head back, glaring at the high ceiling. A sharp pain was forming between his eyebrows again. "I suppose that's for me?"

Kelle's voice was apologetic. "That was security calling from the surveillance room. One of your lower levels is panicking. It's like an army of Tasmanian devils is scurrying about."

Rhys held his breath until his lungs burned before releasing it. Exiting the office, Quin chuckled and elbowed him. "This is what I meant about the movie clichés."

"I need to get someone trained…fast."

A look of realization crossed Quin's expression. "Wait a minute. Didn't Ivan use to have some guy working with him for a bit? Sa…Saw…Sawyer? I think that's it. Romeo or Roberto Sawyer — or something like that. I know his name starts with an R."

Kelle frowned as she typed in the name. "No, there's no one with the first or last name Sawyer in this pile."

"That's weird," Quin murmured, scratching his head. "I could've sworn someone brought the name up not too long ago. Said Ivan had some lapdog doing his work while he made his rounds."

Rhys glared in exasperation. "If you're trying to get my hopes up, you're an ass."

Quin grinned, shaking his head. "No, I really did —"

Kelle was rapping at her keyboard again, then clicked the mouse several times. "Well, there's a Remington Sawyer in the reject file. A data entry clerk from the lower floors."

"Yes!" Quin exclaimed with a snap of his fingers. "That was his name — Remington Sawyer."

Rhys stepped forward, leaning over the desk to peer at the screen. "Does he have any qualifications or anything to suggest he studied under Ivan?"

Kelle zoomed in on the typed report. "Yes, actually. It says here Ivan enlisted Remington to train under him dozens of times since he took on the job as COO."

Thorne scoffed. "Sounds like he really conned the poor bastard while he went to slack off somewhere."

Rhys ignored him. "What's his work ethic?"

Kelle scrolled through the rap sheet. "Efficient. Wow. *Very* efficient. Able to work under pressure. Excellent multitasker. Exceptional leadership skills. Lots of compliments. Seems everyone on the lower floors adores this guy."

Rhys lifted an eyebrow. "Well, what the hell is he doing in the reject file, Kelle? He's exactly what I need. Better yet, he already knows how to do Ivan's job."

Kelle scrolled to an attached file with a big red circle and an X stamped across it. "Excessive tardiness and employed under five years. Those are your usual requirements."

Rhys grunted. "Is that all? I suppose that can be overlooked, so long as he proves himself worthy."

"Wait a moment, sir —"

"I don't have the time to look for someone to train, certainly not while I already have a man who knows what he's doing. There would be very little work to do to teach him the full ropes."

"Yes, but, sir —"

"Data entry, you say? That must mean he's on the lower floors with the chaos, too. I'll find him."

"Rhys —"

"No time, Kelle. No time." Rhys was already striding around the corner, passing through the elegant waiting room and toward the bank of elevators. His brothers were on his heels. He walked with a bit more pep in his step as a flare of hope lit within him.

Thorne and Quin didn't say much on the ride down, perhaps not wanting to jinx his luck. With the mood he was in, they were wise not to press him too far.

When the doors opened, Rhys paused when he realized he hadn't the slightest clue what this Remington looked like — or even which level the man worked on. Data entry took up four floors, and they were all so vast that one could get lost if they didn't know their way around. He should have asked Kelle to pull up an image and find out where to start—or send an email to him, but oh well. He didn't have the patience to go back.

When he and his brothers rounded a corner to pass through the cubicle maze, the three of them stopped in shock at the sight before them.

"What. The. Fuck," Thorne breathed.

* * * *

Remi had known her coworkers were immersed in chaos long before she, Silas and Gracie had entered the doors to their office space. Her demon senses weren't the sharpest, but her hearing was refined enough that it could pick up on people shouting with panicked voices. When she strode through the doors, she and her two friends stopped in their tracks.

"Oh, my gods," they murmured in unison.

Remi gawked at the paper scattered all along the floor. Someone was banging on the broken copying machine, three others were running back and forth, participating in screaming matches over some nonsense. Several feet above them, some demon was flying around, flapping his wings and sending more paper into disarray. A group was off in one corner, all pointing fingers and yelling expletives at each other while they argued over who knew what.

It wasn't the first time the office workers had gone into panic mode, but Remi had never seen it happen so fast. Everything had been pretty sane before she'd gone on break, which had been just short of an hour ago.

When someone ran past them in a blur of speed, Remi backed away to avoid being crashed into. However, the person was running far too fast to halt in time and ended up slamming into someone who was running in the opposite direction. Upon impact, dozens of papers went swirling into the air and both demons fell to the ground. They jumped to their feet, screaming and cursing before breaking out into a fist fight.

Remi rolled her eyes, stepping several feet away from the melee. She'd already finished the majority of the paperwork on her desk and was going to help the others finish theirs, but with Ivan no longer around, there was nowhere for everyone to turn their final reports in to, which in turn had caused their jobs to get backed up. This was the very thing she'd hoped wouldn't happen. It was like a traffic jam that had come to a full stop, and the more cars lined up, the worse the blockage would be.

Only this traffic jam was turning violent.

"I've never seen them get this crazy before," Silas commented, taking a deep puff from his inhaler.

Remi shook her head in dismay. "Neither have I. Is that… Is that girl over there crying?"

Gracie turned her eyes in the direction Remi indicated and scoffed. "Yes, while hiding under her desk. What a fucking chicken."

Silas shuffled closer to Remi. "Well, Miss I-Secretly-Run-This-Entire-Unit, what are you going to do?"

Remi cocked a brow. "I'm just a data clerk. This is above my pay grade."

Silas and Gracie gave her disbelieving looks. "You're just going to let this continue?"

She shrugged. "I should."

Gracie chuckled. "But you're not going to. That's not you."

Remi shook her head again. "No, it's not."

Drat it all, but she hated seeing things so out of order. Despite her being late for work almost every morning—*I can't help it!*—she was very meticulous about being organized and put together. And she had an endless amount of patience. With parents like hers, it had been necessary, otherwise she would have lost her mind a long time ago.

Raising her thumb and index finger to her lips, she let out a loud, piercing whistle that lasted a good six seconds. At once, everyone in the large room stopped in their tracks. Even the two demons who had gotten into a brawl paused, the one on top holding his fist steady as he was about to deliver another blow to his opponent's bruised face.

Remi spoke in a loud tone, keeping her voice stern. She began barking orders, pointing to several different people at a time to give them something to do. Within moments, everyone was assigned a task and swiftly—yet quietly—began to carry them out. Only a couple paused to glance at her.

"Where should we put all the reports?" someone asked in a mouse-like voice. "Ivan is gone, and his office is already filled with leftover paperwork from the last few days."

"Yeah," someone else chimed in. "If we pile any more in there, there will be no way to sort through it all, and if it becomes jumbled—"

"Don't worry about Ivan's paperwork," Remi said with confidence to calm their nerves. "I will organize it until a new COO is assigned." She pointed a finger at someone passing by. "You three, gather everyone's finalized reports, separate them into folders based on dates and death classifications then place them into one big box. When that's done, bring them to Ivan's office. Okay?"

All three demons looked between one another and nodded, relief settling on their faces. "Got it."

As they scurried along, Remi sighed. Someone patted her on the back. "You done good, Remi," Gracie said with sympathy. "You done good."

Remi snorted. "Yes, but I just signed myself up for pulling several all-nighters to separate Ivan's freaking paperwork." She gave a helpless lift of her hands. "The jerk could have at least had the decency to finish his latest work before quitting. How inconsiderate."

Silas took another puff of his inhaler, the scent of vodka mixed with some kind of fruit tickling her nose before disappearing. "Well, Gracie and I are here to help. Emotionally, anyway. You couldn't pay me to touch a single sheet of paper from his office."

That mindset was shared among almost everyone in the SDC. One teensy tiny mistake would land someone a front-row seat before of Hades, and that was only if the perpetrator survived a terrifying encounter with Damien Lucifer first. Though he was retired, he was still the ruler of Elysium, therefore any mistake made by EUC—the company that his region was built around—was a direct insult to him.

Gracie sucked in a sharp breath, making Remi turn to her. "What is it?"

She pointed a slender finger across the room, stars dancing in her baby blues. "It's all three Lucifer brothers. Gods above and below! What a time to be alive."

Remi craned her head to where Gracie indicated, her heart stuttering when she saw three men standing near the opening of the opposite side of the room—three large, drop-dead gorgeous men she was sure she'd never seen before.

Well, that wasn't true. She'd seen distant portraits of the long line of Lucifers hanging on the halls in the lobby, but a picture could only paint so many words. The real deal was…*wow. Just wow.*

The one in the middle, though, was who caught and held her attention. Despite being a bit more slender in size and an inch or two shorter than the others, he had a certain air of authority that screamed 'I-run-this-shit'. If her gut was correct, that would make him Rhys Lucifer, the eldest brother.

And the CEO of this entire unit.

Remi's ultimate boss of bosses.

His eyes were hard as he scanned the room with a cold calculation, no doubt pissed at the chaotic disarray around them. Though she'd never met the man, she'd heard plenty of stories about how ruthless he was. If something wasn't running the way it should, a handful of people wound up fired on the spot—no warnings, no write-ups, nothing.

A cold lump formed in her stomach. "Let's get back to work before they snap at us," she whispered.

"Good idea," Silas murmured, though his eyes were still pinned on the brothers with open admiration.

Remi shuffled past him and half-crouched, half-walked to her desk. Good gods, had they been standing there the entire time? She hoped not. She didn't want them thinking she thought of herself as some high-and-mighty worker who got off on telling others what to do, nor did she want to draw attention to herself in the event her boss pieced together her name and background. Though her surname was common enough in Sheol and nothing about her or her family's company would pop up on Boogle, the official online search engine in the underworld, she didn't want to take the chance of him digging into her past.

Remi sank into her chair and turned on her computer screen, ducking her head to try her best to disappear among the others ambling around. She prayed the walls of her cubicle would keep her hidden. She only had a handful of papers to finish before setting to work on Ivan's. Hell, if there was any luck at all on her side, she wouldn't have to bother. The three Luci brothers could tackle his paperwork in no time, thus eliminating the need for her to step up and do so.

Maybe she could get Gracie or Silas to ask the brothers if that was what they were going to do. She refused to approach them herself.

Coward? Me? Nah.

Besides, those two were drooling at the mouth to have a reason to speak to one of the infamous devils. It was a win-win situation for everyone.

With that thought in mind, she started to lean around the corner of her wall but paused when the hairs on the back of her neck stood on end. The top of the database app she was using had a black strip of settings, and in the faint reflection of the screen, she saw someone dressed in a business suit standing behind her. Had she not, however, she would have noticed the rich scent of some sweet cologne and brandy that only a person of vast wealth could afford encompassing her.

Pretending not to notice him would be pointless, of course. She'd already gone still and a nervous bead of sweat had formed at her temple. Devils had the ability to read others' body language, inner feelings and ever-shifting moods. They were masters at detecting even the subtlest of emotions. She didn't doubt for one moment that the Lucifer behind her could sense her discomfort.

Inhaling his heady scent, she straightened her shoulders and swiveled her chair around to face him.

From a distance, Rhys Lucifer was a very handsome man. Up close? *Sweet gods and goddesses…* Hair cut short and brushed away from his face, molten brown eyes framed by lush lashes, square jaw and fine-cut features… It didn't help that he was tall with a lean chest, had shoulders tapering to a narrow waist and long legs, all encased in an expensive, hand-tailored blue suit atop a crisp white shirt and dark blue tie.

Remi had seen handsome men before. She'd even seen beautiful men, in Sheol and topside. However, she couldn't recall a day in her life when she'd ever seen someone who sent a scorching heat tingling through her body with just a glance. Her lower stomach clenched and dampness pooled at her core, the result of a combination of his exotic aroma and the sinful upward tilt of his lips. Her reaction to him was shocking and unprofessional, making her scold herself.

Surprise flickered in Rhys' eyes, though Remi couldn't say she knew what about. Then, embarrassment slid through her at the notion that he could sense her arousal.

Good gods below, please don't let that be it, she thought as she tried to keep heat from rising to her cheeks. *Please let there be a pimple on my face or lipstick staining my front teeth. Please.*

Remi supposed she'd never know the truth behind his surprise, because his features relaxed into a small smile of greeting that didn't quite reach his hard eyes. "Good afternoon. Rhys Lucifer." He held out his hand to her.

She eyed it, a shiver dancing down her spine as her mind offered images of the wicked things that big appendage could do to her. Schooling her expression to be what she hoped was cool professionalism, she stood and shook his hand. His engulfed hers, feeling rough and smooth. Velvet over stone. She wondered if other parts of him would feel the same way.

Down, girl, she chided.

"Remington Sawyer," she murmured in response. "Data entry clerk."

His eyes widened as he gave her a once-over. "*You're* Remington? The one who's been training under Ivan?"

Remi frowned, pulling her hand from his lingering touch. It was far too distracting. "I wouldn't call it training, sir. Just…lending a helping hand."

He made a dismissive motion with his hand. "But you know how to do his job."

Remi frowned, narrowing her eyes a fraction. She did not like where this was going. At. All. "I know the basic ropes."

That was a lie. Even the COOs before Ivan had enlisted her help on multiple occasions, offering her promotions and whatnot in exchange for her silence on the matter.

"I see," Rhys murmured with delight. "Well, Miss Sawyer, you're just the person I was looking for. I'd like to extend an invitation for you to join me in my office upstairs. I have much I wish to discuss with you."

Remi stifled a groan, instead giving him a single nod. "Certainly, sir." She waved toward the small stack of folders lying across her desk. "However, I'll need a little time to complete these worksheets first."

Rhys spared the neat pile a brief glance before nodding. "Very well. I'll see you within…an hour."

Remi just nodded. Rhys flashed another half-smile before returning to his brothers across the room. When they walked out of sight, Remi flopped down in her seat with a loud groan.

Silas and Gracie peeked around the corner. "Girl, do you know what this means?" Silas asked with excitement.

Gracie was grinning. "Other than the fact that Remi is the luckiest fucking person in the world to have some alone time with Rhys Lucifer? She's about to become our boss!"

Remi grunted. "Stop it, you two. I have no intentions to become COO or anything more than what I am."

"Well, what are you going to do if he offers you the position? You can't just say no to him."

"Why not? I've said it to Cleveland and Tierre when they offered to promote me. I'll just decline and say I'm not ready or something. He can't force me to accept a promotion — if that's what he even wants from me."

Gracie sighed, scooting her chair out of sight as she continued her paperwork. "I still say you should go for it. At least give it a test run."

Remi snorted, also continuing her work. "I've been giving it a test run since Cleveland first asked me to help him three years ago. It's not for me."

Silas took a long puff of his inhaler. "You'll change your mind soon enough."

Chapter Four

"Something on your mind, brother?" Quin asked from the middle of Rhys' office.

Rhys glanced up from where he sat behind his desk. "What?"

Thorne nodded at Rhys. "You've been fidgeting with your tie for the past thirty minutes."

Rhys peered down to find that he was indeed working at the knot of his tie, loosening and retightening it. He frowned, pulling the accessory free and returning it to its immaculate state. "I suppose I'm just a bit distracted with everything going on."

Thorne and Quin shared an amused look. "Perhaps it's something to do with that hot redhead downstairs?" Thorne questioned with a wide grin.

Rhys' frown deepened and an odd heat flared within him. When he'd seen Remington from across the room, he'd been impressed. The woman had exuded cool confidence, and what was more surprising was that there was no hesitation among the other workers on the floor. They'd followed her orders and, within minutes, the entire floor had resumed its calm atmosphere, as everyone worked together to clean the lingering mess.

No one had even noticed that all three Lucifers had been watching the scene play out.

Rhys had forgotten his purpose for being on that floor as he'd made his way to meet the woman and find out how she'd managed such a feat so swiftly. He knew all his managers, and she definitely wasn't one of them. He would have remembered.

Upon seeing her up close, he'd felt like he'd just been sucker-punched in the gut.

Remington Sawyer was a very beautiful woman, and he'd been blown away by that knowledge. Tall and leggy with an hourglass figure outlined by the tight black skirt she wore, she had a mane of flaming red hair that had been pulled into a thick braid that fell halfway down her back. Bright hazel eyes had danced between shades of green and brown, full pink lips complemented her fair, flawless skin and, though she'd forced a smile at him, he'd caught a flash of straight white teeth.

When he'd read her body language, he'd known she was tense, but he hadn't missed her brief flare of arousal when he shook her hand. Everything about her had caught him off guard, but it was his own body's response that shocked him. Just from her heated look, his muscles had tightened with the desire to lean closer to her. All the blood had rushed straight to his groin, the neglected organ half-stiffening in his pants.

Even an hour later his body felt...strange, as if he'd downed an entire pot of coffee with extra shots of espresso. His blood was racing, his body buzzing with activity that made it hard for him to sit still. He placed his hand on his thigh to keep it from bouncing up and down. *What the hell is wrong with me?*

"Bro?" Thorne asked, knocking on the edge of his desk. "You good?"

Rhys blinked again, shaking his head to clear it. "What?"

Quin stepped forward, shoving his hands into his pockets. "Damn, brother, did she put a spell on you or what?"

Rhys grunted, reaching deep for the calm composure he was known to have. "It's the stress of the bullshit I've been dealing with," he muttered. "The Séance Convention is less than two weeks away, I have to train someone new to take over as my chief operating officer and fix the shit Ivan left behind, I have twelve different meetings to go to in less than a week and, to top it all off, I have about four more months to find a suitable wife before Elysium is given to the Belials. So no, I'm not all that good right now."

His brothers just shared another look with each other, both of them already aware of the threat hanging over their family's name.

Before Sheol had been divided into four regions, there had only been two — Elysium and Abyssia. Their great-plus-grandfather had always had a rivalry with the Belials, the family in charge of Abyssia. To end the constant fighting over territory boundaries and other petty arguments, Hades had deemed it so that every first-born of the family's head, whether it be a son or daughter, must take a mate by their hundredth birthday to secure their lands. Should a first-born fail to do such a thing, the region would be gifted to the opposing family.

Even long after the older Lucifers had divided Elysium into two more regions, The Meadows and Asphodel, the fighting had only been between the Lucifers and Belials. The other two families had stayed out of it, though it was no secret that they didn't care for the conniving Belials either.

Damien Lucifer had taken a wife almost a thousand years before, but they hadn't had any children until Rhys ninety-nine years ago, then Quin and Thorne.

Rhys had put off finding a wife for as long as possible, because he had no desire to settle down. He was always focused on his work, and while he took lovers on occasion, he made sure it was never anything more than that. Emotional attachments weren't his thing, and even when he took a wife, it would be out of duty. He needed a woman who would understand that his job and responsibilities came first. There was no place for a thing such as 'love' in his life, and he had every intention of keeping it that way.

Still, with his hundredth birthday just around the corner and all the other shit going on, he'd be better off letting his father set him up with one of his numerous allies. He was sure whoever the old man picked would be a complacent wife who wouldn't step out of line.

"I'm glad as shit I'm not the firstborn," Quin said.

Thorne nodded in agreement. "Look at it this way… Though the convention is going to be annoying as hell with those other families there, at least the resort we'll be staying in will be kind of like a sweet vacation spot. When we aren't dealing with the pesky meetings, we can tour the city, hit up the local clubs, kiss a few mortal hotties…"

At Quin's green expression and Rhys' disbelieving stare, Thorne sighed. "Oh, right. I'll be with Mr. Clean and Sir Stick-in-the-Mud. I forgot that you two don't know how to have fun anymore."

Rhys leaned back in his chair and tapped one foot. That was true. He couldn't remember the last time he'd gone out for an enjoyable night. The most pleasure he got out of life these days was in a few uninterrupted hours of sleep at night.

And Quin didn't go anywhere there would be a lot of people brushing against him. Clubs and crowded streets were out of the question.

A red light beeped on his desk phone, and Rhys answered it. "Yes, Kelle?"

"Remington Sawyer is here to see you," his secretary said to him. She lowered her voice as if trying not to be overheard. "Before you left, I was trying to tell you that 'he' is actually a 'she'."

Rhys straightened, clearing his throat. "Thank you, but I didn't have to look. Tell her to wait five minutes."

Kelle hung up, and Rhys glanced down at his tie, tugging to make sure it was still in place. He scowled when his brothers snickered. "Something humorous?"

Both of them were grinning, but neither said a word.

His frown deepened and he shooed them toward the door. "If you don't need anything, then leave. I have a private meeting to attend."

"No way, man," Thorne said. "I've never seen you so ruffled over a female. I wanna see how this plays out."

"Ditto," Quin added.

Rhys glared daggers at them. He pointed at the door. "She does not have me ruffled. I have important matters to discuss with her — and the sooner the better. Now… Get. *Out*."

Both men sighed and grumbled until they were outside. Alone, Rhys took the time to smooth his hair back and straighten his suit jacket. He glanced at his reflection in his computer monitor, confirming that nothing was out of place before calling Kelle.

A minute later there was a light, almost hesitant knock on his office door. "Enter," he commanded.

The door opened and Remington Sawyer made her way inside, glancing around. He swelled with pride at the way her eyes widened at the luxurious decorations of his private office. Though he'd consulted with an interior designer on how he wanted the office arranged, the majority of it had been his own tastes and desires, and he'd spent a small fortune getting it to be as comfortable as it was elegant.

Everything from the expensive leather couch and armchairs to the hanging chandelier shedding bright light across the dark carpet and crimson walls with gold accents spoke of wealth—and that was the way he liked it.

With a small smile, Rhys indicated one of the two chairs on the opposite side of his desk. "Thank you for joining me, Miss Sawyer. Take a seat."

She did so, each step giving off the same cool, confident vibe he'd seen when she was giving out commands to her coworkers.

He waved toward the minibar off to one side of the room. "Before we get started, can I offer you a beverage?"

She lifted a slim brow. "Thank you, but I don't drink during work hours, sir."

Oh…right.

"Very well," he murmured, refusing to feel foolish over his question. Perhaps she thought he was testing her, but it had been a sincere offer. He clasped his hands together and leaned forward. "Miss Sawyer —"

"Please, call me Remi," she said. She gasped. "I'm sorry. I didn't mean to interrupt you."

Rhys quirked his lips into a small smile, though he couldn't keep his eyes from narrowing a bit. To anyone else, she would have appeared nervous and coy, but Rhys was an experienced devil. He got the feeling it had been forced, as if her feigned innocence was… sarcastic, in a way. Though her eyes were wide and expressive, it was hard to get a precise reading on her.

"Very well. Remi, I suppose you are wondering why I've requested your presence." He lifted the stapled papers laid out in front of him, pretending to scan her rap sheet. He'd read and reread it over a dozen times in the past hour. "I've reviewed your employee file, and I must say you have shown some rather impressive scores in the years you've been here. Besides your tardy record, you're practically a model worker."

She lifted one slender shoulder in a small shrug. "Thank you, sir."

"Rhys," he corrected, though he didn't know why. None of his employees, save for Kelle, referred to him by his first name alone, not even his COO. "Call me Rhys. You have the leading scores among the other clerks, and when they're behind, you pick up the slack. Furthermore, you have several compliments on your work ethic, especially among your peers. It's remarkable.

"With a rap sheet like this, it makes me proud that we in the Soul Distribution Center have such an invaluable employee. You have all of the qualifications to be an excellent leader, and I'm sure that with your help, EUC can achieve an even greater reputation in diligence, efficiency and profoundness. With that being said, I'd like to offer you a promotion. There's a hierarchy ladder to climb, but in this case, I'd like to skip those steps and promote you straight to COO."

Rhys finished his grand speech with a small smile, wanting to pat himself on the back. It was the same speech he'd given to Ivan, Tierre, Cleveland and several others, but unlike with them, he meant his words. After seeing the way Remi had handled the chaos downstairs, he was positive she was different.

If Rhys expected a gasp of surprise, an elated grin or even a frantic *'OMG, this is so unexpected!',* then he was disappointed. Remi regarded him with a bored expression, as if she'd already anticipated him offering her a promotion.

Then, she smiled sweetly. "No thanks."

Rhys smirked, turning to gather a manila folder that contained information for her to fill out. "Excellent. We can begin discussing your pay and benefits, as well as move your things into your new office. With the upcoming…" Rhys trailed off as her simple words sank in. He turned to her, tilting his head in confusion. "I'm sorry. Did you just say 'no thanks'?"

Remi nodded, continuing her sweet smile. "I appreciate the offer, but no thank you."

Rhys parted his lips, closed them, then parted them again. He shook his head. "Do you understand how much of an honor having the title of COO is at this company?"

Remi nodded again, that smile unwavering as she maintained the feigned look of innocence. "I understand perfectly well, sir, but my answer stands."

"But…why not? You'll have your own private office and assistant, and with the pay you'll be making, you could afford just about anything you want."

"I have no desire to deal with the strain that comes with Ivan's job, plain and simple. I'm comfortable and pleased with where I'm at now, and with all due respect, there is nothing that is going to change my mind on it... *Sir*."

Rhys sat back in his chair, flabbergasted. She was blunt and straightforward, and he was positive that beneath her honied smile and polite manner of speaking was an underlying sardonic tone. He didn't know how to react. He hadn't expected her to outright reject the position — and with such certainty. She hadn't even thought it over, which meant she'd been expecting this all along.

Furthermore, if she didn't want the position, then he was back to being stuck with picking out a candidate from the sorry-ass list of 'maybes'. *Gods below, what the hell am I going to do?*

As if able to see his stress level rising, Remi offered, "I get that you're a busy man, Rhys, so while I'm going to have to decline your offer, I can at least tidy up Ivan's office and complete his workload until you find someone to accept the promotion. I'll even help train them, if need be."

Rhys tilted his head to the side, narrowing his eyes. "If you only know the basics of the job, how can you train someone to do it?"

She had a mischievous twinkle in her eyes that contradicted the innocent smile she flashed him. "I lied about that. Sorry. Truth is, I know how to do every aspect of Ivan's job — everything from the paperwork, to distributing the souls, to dealing with employee requests. Your last two COOs have given me some insight on doing the job when they needed help, but Ivan went overboard with it."

He leaned forward once again, intrigued. "So, it's true then? He fooled you into doing his job while he, what? Lazed about?"

She bristled at that, clearly taking offense. "Excuse me? He didn't fool me into doing anything. I only did his work because if he'd kept getting behind, then everyone would resort to panic mode. And believe you me, he did *not* know how to handle that very well."

"So, you accepted the weight of his work in order to keep the peace among your peers," he murmured. She nodded, and Rhys' admiration for her went up a notch. How often did he come across someone who was so dedicated to their fellow coworkers that they took extra responsibilities just to help them?

Never.

Rhys drummed his fingers across the top of his desk. Remington Sawyer was unlike anyone he'd ever encountered before — work-wise, anyway. She was the exact type of person he needed as his COO, and the fact that she already knew how to play the part made him more eager than ever to promote her.

Unfortunately, she seemed dead-set on declining the offer. He needed someone now, and here was the perfect employee sitting across from him, but she was refusing, despite the benefits outweighing the cons. If he could just have a little bit more time to convince her…

With a sudden thought, Rhys straightened in his seat. "Okay, Remi, I have a proposition for you." When she grew cautious, he held up a passive hand. "Just hear me out. In ten days, my brothers and I, as well as others from our sister corporations in the neighboring regions, will have to attend an annual Séance Convention topside. This convention is mandatory for all the heads of EUC, CEP, IM and Bell Towers, and each is encouraged to bring their highest-ranking employees. This is a weeklong event in which we all get together and share ideas, successes, concerns, yearly reports and several other things. Since Ivan is no longer with us and I have no time to teach someone everything they need to know about his position in a ten-day time frame, I would like for you to accompany me in his stead."

She frowned. "You want me to act as a stand-in COO?"

"Only until I can give someone else the position. Since you already know the ropes, it would be appreciated on my end if you could accept it as a temporary situation. After the convention ends, I will select someone to take the job and you can train him or her." He paused to give her a minute to soak in the information. "Of course, this is a large request I'm asking of you, but I am more than willing to pay you large bonuses should you accept — one for completing Ivan's tasks for the next ten days, one for attending the convention for the week and one for training the next COO."

She was quiet for several minutes, her eyes lowered as she thought it over. Rhys opened his devil abilities to try to get a reading on her emotions, but once again, they were hard to understand. It was almost as if she was able to disguise them from him, giving him only glimpses. It shouldn't have been possible, since devils had the greatest senses for seeing others' inner feelings. And since the brief flashes he was able to detect from her were all negative, he was sure she was going to decline the offer again.

To his surprise, though, she said, "Where is the convention going to be located?"

Rhys lifted his brows. "Miami Beach, Florida. Do you know where that is?"

Remi thought it over before nodding, her shoulders relaxing with an odd sense of relief. Rhys was confused. He wondered what she was hiding in that pretty little head of hers. "If you can promise me that this is only temporary and you will find someone for me to train as *soon* as the convention is over, then I'll accept your proposition."

Rhys let out a small breath he hadn't realized he'd been holding. He gave her a genuine smile, because little did she know that he had every intention of spending the entire time convincing her to become his permanent COO.

And if he were lucky, he was going to get at least a little taste of the wicked mischief lurking deep in her eyes before then. His dick had been standing at half-mast since he'd first seen her, pitching a tent in the front of his suit pants. One small quickie with the pretty vixen should clear that right up.

"We have a deal then, Miss Sawyer."

Chapter Five

Remi couldn't help but think she'd sold her soul to the very devil as she came in to work the next morning—a rather fitting description, given she'd accepted the position of Rhys Lucifer's right-hand for the next two and a half weeks.

She wished she could say it had only been for the money, that the bonuses would be a great help to her financial situation. However, that would be a lie.

For one, her body had gone against her and decided that getting physically close to her sexy devil boss wouldn't be all that bad. The man looked like he knew a thing or two about pleasing a woman, and damn the gods if she wasn't interested in testing that theory. As she'd sat across from him in his office, all she'd been able to think about was climbing over the massive desk and straddling his lap.

For two, she was...curious. At the mention of the Séance Convention, she'd perked up like a puppy offered a treat. It had been many years since she'd gone topside, and she longed to feel the sun's rays on her skin again.

So, an all-expense-paid, weeklong stay on the bright and sunny coast of Florida? Besides having to attend the convention, that sounded like a lovely vacation to her. No way was she passing that up.

She'd just have to be careful not to reveal her powers during her stay, however.

All demons were from Sheol, so they were at their strongest in the underworld realms. Visiting the human world drained them of their powers, leaving them weak and tired after prolonged exposure. It was the entire reason the annual conventions were ruled to take place there, in the event that one or more of the regal families decided to have an all-out brawl. They could only go at it with their fists, so that way there were no fatalities that would result in another war.

Remi, however, was one of the very rare few demons who was an anomaly. Her mother was a demon but her father was a powerful shaman, a human born with magical powers. It was because of his blood that Remi was strongest topside, while being in Sheol made her…well, mortal-ish. She couldn't use her full powers — *not that I've needed to anyway* — and while that itself wasn't a crime, there were always those darker demons lurking that wouldn't hesitate to use someone like her for their own personal gain, especially if they found out who her parents were.

With a small shake of her head, Remi made her way to Ivan's former office. She was aware of the whispers among her coworkers, of the wide-eyed stares they were giving her as she passed through. It didn't take a mind reader to know what they were thinking — that she'd been promoted to COO. While it was the second highest ranking position in this entire division, only someone who was really brave or really stupid would take on such a job. Even those of upper ranks who were next in line wouldn't have wanted it.

Ivan had been a transfer recruited from The Meadows, which was home to one of their sister corporations, Infernal Meadows. He'd been so sure he could take on the requirements of the job, and while there was nothing wrong with having confidence, the man had been arrogant, acting all high-and-mighty on his first day. And just as it had been with the others, he'd gotten far more than he'd bargained for. After the first month, the change within him had started. Dark circles had formed under his eyes and his attitude had grown from haughty to downright snippy. From there, it had been a seven-month downhill slide until he'd snapped.

Remi approached the office door, sucking in a deep breath before pushing it open. As expected, the large room was a mess, with tall stacks of paper lining the floor. Someone had had the decency to label them by date, which made organizing them somewhat easier. Still, she was in for quite a long day—several days, actually. Hell, it was going to take about a week to sort through it all before catching up the most recent reports.

Thanks for nothing, Ivan, she groaned to herself.

With a sigh, she closed the door and went to work.

* * * *

Remi didn't bother glancing up at the sound of someone knocking at the door. After working nonstop since clocking in, she had a laser focus on the task at hand. "Come in," she ordered, still checking off numbers from the paperwork and onto the computer screen.

"You're still here?"

The surprised voice rolled over Remi, making her pause as it sent light tingles throughout her body. She peered up at Rhys, pretending the heat pooling in her girly bits was from her eagerness to eat lunch. "Did you think I would go back on my word?" she questioned.

His lips quirked into a small smile. "No, but I didn't think you'd be so dedicated as to work well into the night."

Remi frowned. "Well into the night? It's only noon…" She trailed off as she took notice of the time located in the corner of her computer. Eight-fifteen p.m. EUC had closed its doors and offices three hours before, and only the cleaning crew stayed this late. "Wow, I hadn't realized so much time had passed." Her frown deepened as she scanned the piles in the room. Not even a quarter of the work had been done because she'd been delayed due to going back and correcting Ivan's previous mistakes in the system.

"Have you eaten lunch?" he asked.

She shook her head, tucking a stray curl behind her ear. "I thought it *was* lunchtime, so no."

He nodded his head toward the door behind him. "Let's go grab some dinner."

"Erm…no, that's okay." She saved the current data she was working on and shut the computer off, picking up her purse and slinging the strap across her shoulder as she stood. "I always take the bus home, so—"

He lifted an eyebrow. "The nearest bus stop is a quarter of a mile down the road. It's rather dangerous to be out this late, isn't it?"

What's more dangerous is the fact that I want your face between my legs, a voice called out in her head.

Remi gave him a wry smile. "We *are* in hell, Rhys. Can't get much more dangerous than that."

Amusement lit his eyes. He jerked his chin over his shoulder. "Come on. I'll give you a ride. And dinner is my treat." For an added measure, he tossed in, "After all, since we'll be working close together for the next few weeks, don't you think it wise for us to become better acquainted?"

Remi chewed her bottom lip as she thought it over. There was a silent promise in his casual words. Or maybe that was her sex-deprived inner voice conjuring up all types of images of how they could become 'better acquainted'. She couldn't help but think Rhys had some kind of ulterior motive and that the sexy grin on his face was nothing but trouble.

Still, she was starving, having only eaten a granola bar earlier.

If she were being truthful, a tiny piece of her was curious to learn more about her handsome boss. So long as she didn't reveal too much about herself, where was the harm in going with him?

Besides, it wasn't like it was a date or anything, just two coworkers getting dinner to discuss business plans and ideas—nothing more, nothing less. Although, she had to admit, if only to herself, that it would be nice if he accepted an invitation into her home for some *dessert*.

"Well?" he prodded, impervious to the inner war going on in her brain.

Remi allowed a tiny smile to curve her lips. "I *am* a bit peckish. I could go for a bite." She trailed her eyes down his tall frame in a way that would let him know the feeling went beyond food.

He got it. Remi caught the flare of heat in his eyes, as if her 'innocent' words had turned him on. She even noticed a small twitch below his waist, which had her tongue going dry. His reaction was shocking, but he did well to hide it as he turned and waved a hand to let her exit first.

Like a true gentleman, she acknowledged.

It crossed her mind that the man could very well fire her for sexual harassment had they been topside, but demon corporate policies weren't as strict in Sheol. Sex was the most basic of primal needs for the majority of demons. So long as everyone did their work in a timely fashion, no one batted an eye at the fact that a *lot* of people in all three divisions of EUC would oftentimes sneak off to have a quickie in a private closet, office or the elevators. Even the Lucifers, namely Thorne, were known to have casual encounters with their own employees.

Walking past him, she inhaled his rich scent, feeling her insides quiver at the sheer deliciousness of him. Gods below, the man was dangerous. His looks, his smell, his smile… Everything about him made her want to pull him into the office, clear the desk of the mountain of paperwork and have him ravish her right then and there.

One casual hookup wouldn't be so bad. She was single and hadn't had sex in months, and she wasn't looking to fall in love. Plus, she knew full well he was just as turned on by her as she was by him. She didn't have a devil's ability to sense others' emotions, but she was a half-djinni, which meant she was able to 'see' when someone wanted something in their hearts.

And deep in Rhys' heart, she was picking up on some fuckable vibes. The only thing left to do was to pull on those feelings until she could convince him to put them both out of their misery.

As expected, the ride down the elevator to the underground parking garage was silent. Remi clutched the strap of her purse to keep from fidgeting with her hair or tapping her foot to break the silence. Meanwhile, Rhys was the perfect image of calm. His hands were tucked into his pants pockets while he waited, until they arrived on the garage floors. He then led the way to his private parking space where — *surprise, surprise* — a brand new Mercedes-Benz with a shiny white coat of paint and clean black rims waited for him.

He held the passenger door open. Remi murmured her thanks and settled into the seat, the fresh scent of pine needles and new car filling her nose. Rhys settled into the driver's seat and exited the parking garage to head into the city.

Though it was always nighttime in the underworld, it was clear to all demon residents which was considered morning and which was night. Like any large city topside, cars flitted about, crowding the streets as the night owls traveled around. Rhys weaved his way in and out of traffic, turning onto several streets until they reached the 'high-brow side of town,' as Gracie would say, a half-hour later.

"Where are we going?" Remi asked, having never traveled this far from her apartment. She didn't live in the slums, that was for sure, but her average-sized, two-bedroom flat could never fit among the fancy buildings meant to provide the utmost comfort to the highest paying customers.

"*Marino Cucina*. Ever heard of it?" When Remi shook her head, he smiled. "It's an Italian restaurant I've frequented for years. The food is"—he kissed his fingertips—"*molto delizioso*."

Remi chuckled at that. "What makes you think I like Italian food?"

He sent her a surprised glance, as if the thought had never even crossed his mind. Then he smoothed it over into a relaxed smile. From the tight lines easing on his face, Remi got the impression he didn't smile very often. "I suppose I should have asked first, but *everyone* likes Italian food. It's magnificent."

"When cooked right." She laughed.

Rhys grinned at her, pulling in the front of a two-story building. Two men wearing valet uniforms rushed to open their doors.

Remi followed Rhys up a small set of stairs and through the open entrance door. A hostess flashed a warm smile at Rhys. "Welcome back, Mr. Lucifer," she purred, observing him with open interest. Remi wasn't even insulted that the woman ignored her existence. Rhys was a gorgeous man. *What woman in her right mind wouldn't be distracted by him?*

The hostess led them through the dining area, where couples and groups sat at round tables with beautiful ornaments adorning the tops. Remi hid a chuckle at the way the hostess swayed her hips with more force than was necessary, trying to entice the devil.

They ascended a larger set of stairs to a quieter, more private part of the restaurant. Despite her earlier words to herself, it felt like a date. Only it was the most elegant date she'd ever been on, and she felt out of place wearing a pair of khaki pants and a plain white blouse.

Rhys pulled her chair out for her, and she thanked him as she sat down. Before he took a seat, he glanced at the hostess, who was smiling and toying with a lock of her hair. "Tell Marino I'll need a bottle of..." he trailed off, his eyes meeting Remi's before returning to the younger woman. "Sangiovese. The oldest one on his shelf."

The hostess nodded and went off to do as asked, though she made sure to brush her shoulder against Rhys as she sauntered off. Rhys took a seat across from Remi.

"You certainly have your pulls, don't you," she drawled.

Rhys grinned, flashing a set of beautiful teeth. "I mentioned this is one of my favorite restaurants. The owner is a good friend of my father's, so they treat me and my brothers well."

"Wow. Being a Lucifer must get you a lot of street cred around these parts."

He tilted his head to the side. "I beg your pardon?"

She chuckled. "You're well-known is all I meant."

"Ah, well of course."

Their waiter came with a dark bottle of wine. After ordering their food, Rhys moved to pour it into both of their glasses.

"Did you get red wine because of my hair?" she asked him, then took a sip.

One corner of his lips tilted upward. "I suppose the inspiration just hit me." He took a gentle taste of his own. "I must say that I was rather shocked to see you made it to work on time this morning. You were even a half hour early."

Remi gave an easy shrug. "I had a lot of work to do and catch up on. Had I been late, I wouldn't have been able to make as much progress as I did today." She paused, then rolled her eyes. "Well, not that it did much to lessen the paperwork."

"Something is better than nothing. I have two meetings tomorrow morning and a luncheon to attend, but afterward, my schedule should be clear. I'll stop by to check on you and assist with what I can."

"That's kind of you, but you don't have to. Really, it's just a matter of stamping and —"

Rhys held up a hand. "It's fine. An extra set of hands couldn't possibly hurt, now could they?"

Remi pursed her lips. "Shouldn't you use that time to search for your next COO?"

Rhys leaned back in his chair. "There's plenty of time for that. Right now, I'm more concerned with getting through the current paperwork to keep the flow steady before another riot breaks out among my workers."

It made sense, but Remi couldn't help but feel Rhys was hiding something. Taking a long drink of her wine, she scrutinized him. "Why do I get the feeling I'm a mouse being toyed with by a lion?"

Rhys let out a hearty laugh, throwing his head back. Remi admired his exposed neck and his chin, clean-shaven and strong. She wondered if he was well-groomed everywhere else underneath that expensive suit.

Then the image of Rhys sitting naked across from her flashed in her mind. She downed the rest of her wine and reached to refill it. She wasn't a lightweight who couldn't handle alcohol, but she was almost certain this particular wine was stronger than most others. All the man had done was laugh and she was ready to crawl under the table and give him another reason to throw his head back.

Gods, she needed to get laid. ASAP.

"I wouldn't consider you a mouse, Remi," Rhys said with a smile. "That doesn't seem a fitting description for your personality."

"Oh?" Remi took a sip of her drink, pretending her body wasn't threatening to melt for this man. She set the glass down and leaned forward on her elbows. "You only met me yesterday. How do you know what my personality is?"

"Hmm." He copied her move, leaning forward enough for his scent to wash over her. "I'm still figuring you out, Miss Sawyer. However, based on what I know about you thus far, you give off this air of quiet serenity, giving others the first impression of coyness — like a mouse. But it's just a façade. In truth, you have a way of saying what's on your mind, yet you choose your words so that they have multiple meanings, which leaves one wondering what it is you're truly thinking about. Along with that, you are a natural leader with a commanding tone that could persuade others to do your bidding and inspire them to follow you. A mouse couldn't possibly have those traits, now could it?"

Remi's heart lurched at his smooth words. For several long moments they stared across the table at one another. His eyes were filled with the same type of heat that was coursing through her body. Something warned her to be wary, that he was a Lucifer — a devil who was a master of seduction and manipulation.

Arguing against it was a separate voice that whispered all the wicked things he could do to her, that her body could use a night of seduction — or two, or three. She wasn't a prude, that was for damn sure, but she'd been so focused on work that she hadn't had any interest in seeking out a relationship — physical or otherwise. Yet ever since meeting Rhys the day before, she was *definitely* interested in developing a physical one.

The waiter broke up the intense staring contest as he placed their food before them. Remi's eyes went wide, her mouth salivating at the delicious scents wafting up to her nose. She'd ordered a salmon dish with a side of some kind of creamy pasta. Good gods below, her stomach growled in appreciation at the sight before her.

Without waiting on Rhys, she dug her fork into both, closing her eyes on a soft moan as bursts of flavor exploded in her mouth. It tasted even better than it looked. She would have to remember to tell Silas and Gracie about this place so the three of them could pay a visit some time. The food, the décor, the manners of the workers — it was all stupendous.

When she opened her eyes, her breath caught in her throat at the way Rhys was watching her with hungry eyes. He licked his lips. "What do you think?" he asked, his voice lower than it had been a moment ago.

Remi swallowed. "It's just as you said…delicious."

"Good." He cleared his throat and went to work eating his own food, chewing slowly as he watched her. Likewise, Remi continued eating, trying — and failing — to contain her pleasure over the tasty food.

They continued in relative silence for the next half-hour, only pausing every so often to exchange small talk, getting to know one another. By the end of the night, when he dropped her off at her apartment, she felt as if a sort of casual air had settled upon them, breaking the formal ice so she could relax around him.

Still, Remi continued to wonder what was on his mind. Because one thing was for certain... He was damn sure on hers.

Chapter Six

"A date?" Silas and Gracie exclaimed.

"Sh-h! Keep your voices down," Remi chided. She glanced past them to make sure the door to her office was closed. It was lunchtime, and, instead of meeting in the cafeteria, she'd invited her two friends to her temporary office. "It wasn't a date."

"Let me get this straight," Silas drawled. "The man gives you a ride, takes you to a fancy, high-class restaurant—and pays—then takes you home and walks you to your door? That sounds like a date to me."

"Agreed," Gracie commented, taking a large bite from her sub. Her eyes twinkled with mischief. "Did you invite him in for *coffee*?"

Remi choked on her own food, knowing full well what her friend meant. "Why on earth would I do that?"

"Why wouldn't you?" Silas counted on his fingers. "He's gorgeous, he's rich, he's a gentleman and he's a freaking devil!"

"And? Am I supposed to sleep with every handsome, rich devil I come across?"

"Yes!" the two yelled. Then, Gracie lowered her voice. "Have you not heard the stories about devils? They're complete sex gods." When Remi snorted in derision, Gracie elaborated. "I'm serious. Devils outrank incubi and succubi when it comes to sexual release."

"That's because incubi and succubi were created *through* devils," Silas informed. "When Hades formed them, he modeled their needs and skills after devils. So, in a way, they really are sex gods."

Remi drank from her bottle of water. "That's all well and good, but I'm still not going to have sex with him. He's our boss. Our *boss*." Even as she said the words, they were an obvious lie. She wanted to jump Rhys' bones like there was no tomorrow, and unless he turned her down, she had every intention of seducing him.

"First off, Thorne has fucked at least thirty percent of the women here, and Quin and Rhys used to do the same once upon a time. You don't hear anyone complaining about those women, do you? No, because no one cares. It's the nature of demons."

"That's beside the point." Remi sighed, taking the last bite of her sandwich. "He only offered to buy dinner to thank me for helping him. Don't read into it too much, because I'm definitely not."

Silas and Gracie looked at each other, then her. "Liar," Silas remarked.

Gracie took a long sip of her drink and pointed at Remi. "Take your hair down."

Remi frowned. "Why?"

"You said he's coming to help you after lunch, right? Give him some eye candy to look at while you work together."

"Eye candy? We're just going to work, guys. Nothing else."

"Right. Keep telling yourself that."

Remi lifted her eyebrows. "Why do you even care? You have your own sex lives to focus on."

Gracie threw her hands up. "I'm going through a dry spell, and Silas over here has decided once again to be 'abstinent'." She used air quotes on the last word, eliciting a snort of humor from Silas. "Be a dear and get some action on our behalf. Your nonchalant attitude doesn't work on us anymore, you know. We know you're dying to know if he's as horny for you as you are for him."

Remi took on a look of mock embarrassment, though she couldn't help the guilty twitch of her lips. She shook her head. "Even if he is, nothing is going to happen. He's my boss, so that means he's off limits."

Silas waved that away, mischief sparkling in his eyes — or maybe it was the hot pink glitter. It was hard to tell. "Right, right. We got it. We just want to satisfy our curiosity, okay?" He tilted his head toward the door, listening for several moments before a wide smile split his face. "Speak of the devil, he's on his way. Come on, Grace."

"I'm serious, guys. I'm not—"

"Bye, Remi. See you after work!" The two gathered their trash and exited the room.

Remi grunted, throwing her own empty bag away. She pulled a small compact mirror from her purse and checked her teeth and makeup, released her hair from its bun and fluffed it a bit. Then, she looked down at her chest and adjusted her bra, pushing her breasts up farther to reveal a hint of cleavage.

She reapplied lipstick to her lips, pursing them to make sure she hadn't used too much or too little. She then replaced the items, breathing a curse when her purse tilted over the edge of the desk, spilling its contents onto the floor.

"Ah, bugger," she complained, bending over to gather the fallen items.

Rhys stepped inside Remi's office, his briefcase in one hand, a bag of takeout in the other. He closed the door, looking down to dig through the bag. "Good afternoon. I brought you lunch if you haven't already—"

His bit his words off when he glanced up at Remi. Instead of walking in to see her sitting behind the large desk, poised and perfect like a model worker, he was instead met with her round derrière facing him while she bent over to pick up whatever was on the floor. Her business skirt was pressed tight against her ass, making him instantly hard.

"Oh! Jeez, I'm sorry," she muttered, straightening with her purse in hand. She turned to him, but that didn't make it any better.

Her fiery red hair was left loose, the curly ends resting over her shoulders and stopping just above her breasts. And speaking of breasts, the neck of her blouse was cut low to reveal a generous amount of cleavage, the creamy white skin making him swallow hard.

Good…lord. All efforts at cool control were tossed out of the window as he drank in the sight of her, using his imagination to peel off every layer of clothing until she wore nothing more than her stockings and heels.

Clearing his throat several times, he averted his gaze to safer territory, like the window behind her that had open blinds to expose the dark sky outside. "I brought you lunch if you haven't eaten already."

"Oh, thank you, but I just finished a few minutes ago."

"Right. No problem. I'll just save this for later." He released the box and set the bag on the waist-high bookcase near the door. He waved toward the desk. "Shall we get started?"

Remi nodded and stepped around the desk. Rhys couldn't help but drop his gaze to her ass again. If he wasn't mistaken, she walked slowly on purpose, swinging her hips to catch his attention. His hand twitched, his mind imagining squeezing the soft flesh. He gave a slight shake of his head, subtly shifting so his hard-on wasn't as evident. Before she could turn around and see the straining erection through his pants, he took a seat in the chair across from her.

He removed his laptop from his briefcase and placed it on the desk, grateful for its large surface area. He cleared his throat again. "How far have you gotten?"

"Hmm..." Still standing, she leaned forward, peering at the clipboard sitting between them. *Gods below*. The vixen had to be trying to seduce him by giving him a deeper view of her breasts. He'd picked up on a few hints she'd thrown his way. And holy fuck if he wasn't tempted to give in. He just had to be positive before his advances scared her away. "I've managed to get us caught up to Monday's souls. We have half of them, then the last two days' worth of souls before we'll be caught up."

Rhys lifted his eyebrows, a smile tugging at his lips. "Very impressive, Remi. I thought for sure we'd at least be a week behind."

Remi sat in her chair. Her red-tinted lips quirked into a sly smile. "We would have been before yesterday. Once I settled into a nice rhythm, everything flowed with ease. It's just a matter of checking to make sure the clerks entered their data correctly before placing the mortals in separate piles for distribution."

Rhys nodded, his mind flashing to Remi's naked body moving above him in an entirely different rhythm. That was what he'd meant when he'd told her she had a way of saying things that were double entendre. While she could say something simple and innocent, the interpretation could in actuality be risqué. And from the smug look in her twinkling eyes, she knew very well what she was doing. He clenched his teeth, his dick stiff in his trousers as the image refused to go away. Gods dammit, he was losing his shit. He needed to focus, not gaze off into space like a horny teen.

He started his laptop and opened the special system only he and his COO had access to. It was a large database that allowed them to file souls away and send them off to the other two corporations for distribution.

"Would you like to listen to some music while we work — or is uncomfortable silence okay with you?" she asked.

Her teasing words made Rhys chuckle. "Could this be any more uncomfortable than when you worked alone with Ivan?"

She considered that before shaking her head. "Good point. He was an ass."

As they'd chatted over dinner last night, Remi had warmed up to him, her manner of speaking shifting to be more casual than formal, something that was pleasing to him. He wanted her to be comfortable around him. It just felt…natural. "Yes, he was. But the man at least knew the inner workings of this job," he said.

She nodded, though her eyes never left the computer screen. "True, but, given the circumstances, I understand why he quit the way he did."

He waited a beat before he commented. "Like the others, he grew overwhelmed with his responsibilities. The wars topside aren't helping matters, as the mortal death tolls increase. Then there was that massive earthquake that struck one of the eastern islands in the Pacific, killing thousands. He got backed up, and instead of asking for help, he just…snapped."

Remi blinked at him. "That's not what I was referring to." At his blank look, she shuffled through the paperwork on the desk before retrieving two papers stapled together. Without another word, she handed them to him and went back to working on her computer.

Rhys glanced over the paper. Instead of names, they used seven-plus digit codes to label each mortal soul. The list was long, some of the codes highlighted yellow, some red and some light blue. "What is this?" he asked, confused.

"Errors," she stated. "Those are a week's worth of souls Ivan was going to send to the incorrect locations."

Rhys took another look at the paper, his jaw going slack. "Are you fucking serious?"

"Quite. So, in a way, it's a good thing that all this paperwork was backed up. Otherwise, I wouldn't have caught the mistakes. And you" — she glanced over at him with a haughty smile — "would have had a massive lawsuit on your hands."

Rhys gulped, because she was right. Seventy-three souls had almost been dispatched incorrectly. *Gods' spit.* If Ivan had sent them out, the Dagons and the Leviathans would have been in an uproar. Not to mention that if word got to Hades about such a large mistake, Rhys, Ivan and half of his workers would have had their asses filleted by one pissed-off god.

No fucking wonder Ivan had snapped. It wasn't because of the work overload. It was because he knew his ass was grass if someone found out what he'd done.

And the bastard was going to leave me to take the fall for it!

"Oh, he is *so* dead when I see him," Rhys growled, dropping the papers to the desk. He scrubbed a frustrated hand over his face, struggling to keep his temper from flaring.

"There's no need to get worked up. The damage was corrected before it became irreversible."

Rhys blinked, studying how calm and refined Remi was. Despite looking ready to be ravished right there on the semi-cluttered desk, she was the very image of sophistication. He was once again struck with the sad realization that such a gem had been working for him for three years, yet he'd never known, never even had a clue. She looked as though she belonged there — as if the stress that came with being COO was nothing she couldn't handle. None of his previous officers had exuded such a vibe, which had him wondering who Remington Sawyer was, where she came from and how she managed to stay so poised and cultured in the midst of chaos. It was as though she were born to run this type of work environment.

"Are you sure I can't convince you to take this position permanently?" he asked, half-teasing. "You're remarkable."

Remi smiled, fluttering her long lashes at the compliment. "I'm sure, but to thank me, you can hold a fun event for your workers from time to time."

Rhys crinkled his forehead in genuine confusion. "Fun event?"

She nodded. "Thorne and Quinn both set aside a weekend once a year to host Olympic-style games for their employees to either participate in or watch. Infernal Meadows has a large company retreat for the employees who have been there for at least a year. The Dagons in CEP have a grand annual carnival they run for their employees and their families. I've even heard that the Belials in Bell Towers host a big block party around Halloween each year."

She stopped typing and faced him. "Even if it's as small as an office holiday party, something is better than nothing. Soul Distribution is the backbone of EUC, after all. Without us, our sister corporations wouldn't exist, and keeping up with the constant arrivals and departures of mortals would thrust you and your family back into the Stone Ages, not to mention be impossible for you all to keep up with by yourselves. Thousands would be unemployed, and you'd have to deal with souls the old-fashioned way, with those horrifying concentration camps. And though none of your employees are willing to complain or say it to your face, I can tell you first-hand how much they would appreciate your personal show of gratitude for their hard work."

In the twenty-plus years since he'd taken over the family business, Rhys had never once thought of such a thing—neither had anyone besides his brothers possessed the balls to be so…direct with him about his own employees. Remi was kind as she spoke to him, but the certainty in her voice told him this was far more than just a friendly suggestion.

And once again, she was right. While his two brothers' domains in EUC were of equal importance to running this company, SDC was the toughest division to work in, and everyone knew it. Yet not once had he ever thought about throwing some kind of 'thank you' celebration.

Furthermore, he had no fucking clue his brothers did their own thing once a year. Olympic-style games? Why had they never mentioned it to him? He had to remember to question them about that later in the evening. *Gods below*, his employees must think he was the coldest boss in the underworld, something that bothered him far more than it should have. While he ruled his company with an iron fist, he was fair and cared about the well-being of his people. "This is certainly something to think about," he murmured, shaking his head. "Why hasn't anyone come to me about this?"

Remi scoffed. "How many people do you think are willing to approach a Lucifer with such a bold request?" She returned to her computer work while she spoke. "Do not take this as me complaining on their behalf, because the people here are comfortable with their jobs. Working in any EUC division is a great honor for them, and they know it. This is just me recommending something that would benefit you. The information is yours to do with as you please…*Sir*."

And so diplomatic. Rhys was learning that Remi had a way of standing up to him and slicing him with her words in the most professional way possible. Worse yet, she could do so with the sweetest smile. The more he thought about it, the more he realized it was quite intimidating.

Intimidating but so damn sexy. Rhys would have never in a million years figured those two could go together on a woman, but here she was only a few feet away from him. The knowledge only made his erection swell further.

He grabbed a packet of papers and began helping with her workload. Suddenly, inspiration struck. Keeping his expression and voice lackadaisical, he said, "You're correct, Remi. It's long past due that I show my gratitude to my employees, but with the amount of work I have to do—you know, as CEO—I just don't have the time. Ivan and the others, of course, never bothered to bring up such a thing with me. I suppose they just…didn't care. About our employees, that is. However, this center would benefit from a leader who cares about them as you do. And employee requests and event planning technically all fall under COO responsibilities…"

Rhys didn't miss the way Remi's moving fingers faltered. He glanced at her. She was watching the monitor with far more concentration than was necessary as she thought about the offer. Then, her full lips curved into a smile that made his dick jump again.

"Your horns are showing," she murmured, continuing with her typing.

Rhys looked down in his lap, thinking for a moment she'd seen he was hard for her. Then he chuckled as he realized she was speaking metaphorically. She knew he was trying to persuade her into accepting the job.

They worked together in companionable silence for a while, making light conversation every so often. Rhys had to admit it was rather nice. Despite the myriad meetings and work waiting for him, he'd made sure to clear this afternoon to 'help' Remi, so she wouldn't be bombarded with the labor. Had it been anyone else, he wouldn't have bothered, but somehow, he'd felt compelled to do so, to be near her.

He was thinking with the wrong head, no doubt. He hadn't had sex in quite a few months, so it wasn't surprising, but his dick chose to remind him of its negligence at the most inopportune times, like since the moment he'd laid eyes on Remi.

The next few weeks were going to be utter madness. Unless…

An idea formed in Rhys' head, a risky one that could end in embarrassment if he wasn't careful. Though Remi was selective about her words and actions, she was making it clear that she wanted him just as much as he wanted her. She just hadn't made a move on him as other women would have.

Though he had a strict personal rule of avoiding sex with employees, he couldn't deny Remi was the sexiest damn woman he'd seen in a long time. Her wit and charm kept him on his toes, and she was always plaguing his mind. He didn't form emotional attachments to anyone, and he'd have to make that clear to her, but so long as it was her, he was willing to dive into a quick round of mindless sex to satisfy the craving she'd awakened in him.

With that thought in mind, he concentrated on their workload for the next several hours, until six o'clock rolled around. Most of EUC would be cleared out by then, with only a handful of stragglers finishing last-minute tasks and whatnot. However, the floor beyond the office was empty. He'd heard the very the moment the last employee had boarded the elevators.

"Let's call it a day," Remi suggested, as if reading his mind. "We've done a good amount."

"Good call." They began to organize the completed papers before shutting their computers off. He packed his laptop and stood. "Regretfully, I won't be free to help much after today. I've already shifted today's meetings to the next few days, so I'll be booked, dealing with those."

Remi nodded in acceptance. "Thanks for helping me today. I can manage the rest on my own."

She wasn't looking at him, instead focused on separating the papers into fresh folders. She leaned forward again, giving him a deep view of cleavage.

"It's no problem," Rhys murmured. "If you need assistance with anything else, I'll do what I can to help."

She turned around to pile the folders into the large filing cabinet behind her, and Rhys' eyes fell to her ass. He licked his lips and tiptoed around the desk to perch on its edge. There was about three feet of space between them.

"Ivan was scheduled to attend a quarterly meeting with the other managers tomorrow morning, so I'll go in his stead. So long as nothing crazy pops up, I should be able to finish everything by Tuesday at the latest," she said.

Rhys didn't say anything, still distracted by the roundness of her perfect ass outlined by her skirt. When she glanced over her shoulder at him, her eyes widened to see he'd joined her behind the desk. She turned around, placing a hand on her hip. He blinked, meeting her amused gaze.

"What?" he asked.

"Were you staring at my ass?" she demanded with a smirk.

Rhys flashed her a charming smile. "I was. It's a nice ass."

"Careful, Mr. Lucifer," she teased. "I can report you to demon resources for sexual harassment."

"What are they going to do? Fire me?"

He'd noticed the first day that her eyes would bounce back and forth between shades of green and brown, the latter taking control every time she became aroused. As they stood a small distance away from each other, those pretty gems were darkening to brown, telling him what he needed to know.

He pushed off the desk, standing to his full height and closing the space between them. He placed his hands on either side of her head, boxing her in between him and the cabinet. "Furthermore, why report me when you want me so badly?"

Her lips parted, her sex perfuming the air and making his dick stiffen. "You don't know what I want," she murmured.

"No?" He leaned in, close enough to have her sweet scent fill his senses, yet still not touching her. Turning his head to whisper in her ear, he said, "You forget that I'm a devil, Miss Sawyer." His breath on her sensitive flesh caused her to shudder, which in turn made him smile. "I can sense everything you feel, and right now you are hot for me."

She made a soft sound somewhere between a sigh and a moan. "Likewise, you've been hard for me since you stepped into this office. Am I right?"

Rhys nipped at her earlobe, eliciting a surprised gasp. "How did you know?" He traced the shell of her ear with his tongue. "I made sure to hide it well."

She tilted her head to the side when he trailed a path of kisses down her neck. "You have your gifts, Rhys, and I have mine."

He wondered what she meant by that but didn't question it further. He didn't want to talk anymore, just feel, because Remi was giving him access to her body, and he had every intention of fucking her until her legs went weak.

He nipped at a spot on her neck and sucked on it, drawing a small moan from her. Still bracing himself with one hand on the file cabinet behind her, he allowed the other to travel over her shoulder to palm one breast through her blouse. It was full and perky, with an erect nipple pressing into his palm through her bra.

Remi's hand covered his, encouraging him to squeeze harder. "Don't be afraid to get rough," she murmured. "I can take it."

Her soft words damn near had him spilling himself right then and there. "I'll show you just how rough I can get," he growled. He gripped her upper arms and spun her around to lean over the desk.

She let out a sound of surprise but didn't protest. She glanced over her shoulder at him with a wicked smile, and damn if she wasn't the sexiest fucking thing he'd ever seen. "Is that the best you can do?" she taunted, waving her ass at him.

"I'm just getting started," he husked, undoing the button holding his pants up. He placed his hands on her rounded cheeks, squeezing before reaching for the edge of her skirt. He shoved it over her waist, revealing bare skin to him. "Good gods, no panties?"

She just winked and laid her head on the desk, watching him with darkened eyes. Rhys spread her lips, the pink petals slick with her wetness. He trailed a finger through her folds and brought it to his mouth, licking her sweetness. Remi sucked in a sharp breath, as if the sight of him tasting her juices turned her on even more.

Rhys grinned and freed himself. He fisted his shaft, sliding his hand from the base to tip, then back down again. Remi said nothing, only watched him over her shoulder with lusty eyes. He used his free hand to toy with her clit while he stroked himself.

"Rhys," she moaned, "please."

"Please, what?" he breathed, picking up the pace on his cock, though he kept his other hand circling her nub slowly. Teasingly. "Tell me what you want, sweet Remi."

"You," she rasped, moving her hips to get his hand to go faster. "I want you inside me."

Rhys pushed her legs apart with his knees, shifting to stand between them. He guided the head of his erection to her waiting dampness, sliding the tip through her slick folds once, twice, then…

"Shit." He sank to the hilt. Remi arched her back, a sound of pleasure escaping her lips as her tight core stretched to accommodate his thick size. "You okay?" he managed to grit out, holding his breath. A bead of sweat rolled down his temple with the sheer amount of control it took to remain still so she could adjust.

"Y-yes," she whimpered. "I told you… I can take it." To prove her point, she pulled away before pushing her ass against him, encouraging him to fuck her.

He blew out a long breath, withdrawing from her sheath before sinking back in. She was so wet. Each time he sank into her, his thrusts picked up speed until the sound of his hips slamming against her ass bounced off the walls. It was the only sound to be heard other than his ragged breathing and her failing attempt to muffle her moans.

Every thrust sent her knees banging into the desk, but she didn't seem to mind as he took her fast and hard. His orgasm was about to hit, but he wanted to satisfy her before then. It had never happened before, this inability to control himself. Remi was so tight that it was hard to refrain. And he'd be damned to Tartarus before he embarrassed himself as a devil by getting off before his partner.

Rhys withdrew from her, eliciting a groan of disapproval. He yanked her to her feet and spun her around to press her back against the nearest wall. Her eyes flew wide when he cupped her ass and lifted her off the ground. She wrapped her legs around his waist and he sank into her once again, pounding her into the wall. She threw her head back and bit her lower lip, her half-lidded gaze revealing red irises.

Damn and double damn. She was so fucking beautiful. Rhys had one hand under her and the other around her waist, holding her close. He leaned forward and placed his lips to her neck, kissing and sucking the tender skin as she gasped and moaned aloud.

"Rhys," she begged, "I'm so close."

"I know," he breathed. He was too. The wetness of their sex squished with each thrust inside her. "You feel so fucking amazing."

She dug her nails into his shoulders as she tensed. Rhys continued to pound into her as her core tightened around his cock, spasming as she rode her climax. Before she was done, Rhys stiffened while his own orgasm tore through him. To keep from shouting out, he bit into her neck, though he was careful not to cause pain. He continued to rock into her until his legs shook.

As they climbed down from the intense peak, Rhys withdrew and set her on her feet. Her legs wobbled, threatening to buckle for several moments before she was able to right herself. "Wow," she breathed, her cheeks stained red from the heat. "I needed that."

Rhys chuckled and moved away, tucking himself into his pants and fixing his clothes. "You and me both."

Remi tugged her skirt in place and used a discarded clamp to pin her thick hair in place. *Pity.* He liked seeing it loose. She straightened her clothes, looking rather sated. Rhys' lips quirked into a smile of male satisfaction. While he shrugged into his suit jacket, she pulled a compact mirror from her purse and wiped away a bit of lipstick that had been smeared near the corner of her mouth. Content with her appearance, she replaced the mirror and tugged her purse onto her shoulder, moving toward the door.

"Thanks again for your help," she said nonchalantly, reaching for the handle.

Rhys lifted an eyebrow. He'd be lying if he said he wasn't a bit wary that she'd want to invite him over for the obligatory post-sex cuddling or go out to dinner or spend more time together. He hated that shit, and though Remi had just given him the best orgasm he'd had in years, if ever, that didn't mean he was ready or interested in moving things to an intimate level.

"You're welcome. By the way, Remi," he called. She half-turned to him. Keeping his voice stern to make her see he was serious, he said, "Forgive me for not saying this sooner, but I'd prefer it if we can agree to keep things purely physical."

She raised her eyebrows in surprise. There was no hesitation, no feeling of longing in her eyes that was a red flag for him to get the hell away from her. There was only a mild sense of gratification, meaning she hadn't fallen hopelessly in love with him yet. She just gave a relieved sort of smile. "Thank the gods you said it first. See you later, boss." With those simple words, she blew him a kiss and walked out of the door.

Rhys just stared after her. *Thank the gods I said it first?* He would have been insulted had he not been pleased that they saw eye-to-eye. He chuckled and picked up his belongings.

Remington Sawyer was nothing like the woman he'd expected, yet she was perfect in every way. It was too bad he couldn't form emotional attachments to anyone. Girlfriends and lovers didn't have a place in his life anymore, not now that he'd be forced to take a stranger as his wife in a few short months. Remi certainly would have been someone he would have taken an interest in to develop a deeper connection.

Rhys shook off the pitiful thoughts, steeling his resolve. There was no sense dwelling on *what if* and *what could be*. This was the life he'd been born into. All he could do was accept it and keep moving forward. Duty came before desire, after all.

Chapter Seven

Remi was bouncing with excitement as she waited for Rhys to pick her up. At last, it was time for them to attend the Séance Convention. Well, the first meeting wouldn't be until the following day, but today they were leaving to go topside, to take a plane from New York to Florida then check into their hotel to relax and explore the city for a while.

The latter was what Remi planned on doing. No doubt oh-so-busy Rhys Lucifer would stay behind and work on whatever it was he did, so she'd be solo. The thought bummed her far more than it should have, but she brushed it off. After five years of living in the dark underworld, she was going to feel sunlight on her skin again, something Florida had plenty of. She couldn't wait.

So, when a knock sounded on the door to her apartment, a wide smile split her face and she darted through her living room to the front door. She threw it open in time to see Rhys still holding his fist up. His eyes widened in surprise.

"Hi," she said, grinning.

He smirked, lowering his hand. "Excited, are you?"

Her stomach tightened, butterflies flying around as she took in his handsome features. Unsurprisingly, he was dressed in a dark tailored suit with his hair brushed from his face. She almost sighed in appreciation before straightening. "Come in. I just have to double-check my purse to make sure I have everything for the carry-on."

She stepped back to allow him to enter. His scent washed over her as he passed by, smelling of aged whiskey and dark chocolate. It was an erotic combination that had her mouth watering for a bite. That mixed with his tall stature, well-groomed appearance and dazzling white smile had Remi's core pooling with heat. Damn, the man turned her on, more so now that she knew he understood how to please a woman.

When Rhys turned to her with a knowing smirk, she hid her reaction by waving a hand toward her couch. "Take a seat. I'll be right back." She rushed past him and entered her bedroom.

Safely tucked away in her own personal space, she released a small groan of frustration. Though she'd seen Rhys only twice during the past week and a half, due to his busy schedule, she'd found her thoughts wandering toward the handsome devil, conjuring up all types of images that involved the two of them naked and replaying the memory of him taking her. Alone, she'd reveled in the mental pornos, and in turn, her sex drive had gone up several more frustrating notches.

Her inability to control her wayward thoughts was coming back to bite her in the ass. They hadn't done anything else since then, nor had they had the time to talk about it.

Then again, what was there to talk about? He'd said he wanted to keep things physical, and she was just fine with that. She wasn't looking to get emotionally involved with anyone, least of all a man with such a highly respected position in their realm. Still, it would be wonderful if he'd be willing to give her another bout of hot, sweaty sex at least once or twice more until the convention was over and he found another COO to take her place.

Jeez, she was starting to feel like a harpy in heat. She needed to cool off. Sure, the man had given her the best damn orgasm of her life, but it had just been to relieve the obvious sexual tension they'd had since they first met.

And he was only working with her because...

Hold the phone. She drew her brows downward and narrowed her eyes while staring ahead of herself. *No freaking way.* Though she had flirted with him to show that she wanted him, it had just crossed her mind that he could have his own intentions of seducing her, to persuade her into becoming his permanent officer. *Gods below, how could I have not seen it sooner?* She was smart about these types of things, always having the upper hand, yet she'd fallen for his easy charm and all but launched herself at him.

She gave a wry laugh, shaking her head as she went through her purse. *Nice going, Rem*, she chided herself. *The man probably thinks he has you wrapped around his finger after that day.*

Ah, well, two can play that game. He might be a master at manipulation, but she wasn't as clueless as he no doubt thought she was. It was going to take far more than delicious, sneaky sex to get her to change her mind.

Remi inhaled a deep breath, held it for several seconds, then let it out, forcing away all thoughts of the devil in her living room. *Focus. Keep it professional. Show him that you're not another mindless bimbo. Do* not *lust after your boss. Do* not *lust after your boss. Do* not...

Yip, yip, yip, yip!

Frowning, Remi opened her eyes. She tilted her head, wondering what squeaking little yips had interrupted her inner pep talk.

"Ow! Son of a bitch!" Rhys yelled.

Then, recalling she'd left the room door adjacent to hers wide open, she gasped and rushed into the hall. She turned the corner and beelined for the living room, only to see her new hellhound puppy yipping away at Rhys.

"Pepper, no! Down, girl," she scolded, crossing over to the little beast who was tugging on Rhys' pant leg with her teeth. Remi grabbed the hound by her pink collar and pulled her away. Despite only being two months old, she was the size of a full-grown English bulldog, and it took more strength to restrain her than Remi would have liked. "Gods, I'm so sorry. This is her first time around guests."

Rhys grunted, cradling his injured hand to his chest. "It's quite all right. I only meant to pet her, but the little creature bit me."

Remi picked Pepper up and carried her to the spare room. She pushed her inside and bolted the large doggy gate in place. She sighed and pushed away from the door when Pepper barked and pawed at it. "She's only two months old, and I just found her a couple of weeks ago, so she's still training."

Rhys' eyes nearly bugged out of his head. "Two months? You're kidding. She bites like an adult."

"Let me see that," Remi said, reaching for his hand.

"Don't worry. It'll heal —"

She ignored him and took his hand in hers, inspecting the wound. Pepper's bite hadn't broken through the skin, thank the gods, but her tiny teeth had left deep indents between his thumb and forefinger. Most demons were immune to the poison of hellhound bites but they were still a bitch to tend to. "Do you need a bandage — or will you survive?"

Rhys snorted. "I'll live," he drawled.

Remi continued to inspect it, admiring how much bigger his hand was compared to hers. His skin was rough and smooth all at once, his nails cut short, though well taken care of. She remembered having that hand smoothing across her skin as it slid down her neck to cup her breasts, then caressing her ass while she was bent over her desk. *Mm-m.*

"Remi?" Rhys asked, his voice low. Dark. Seductive.

Remi tilted her head up at him. His molten eyes were threatening to pull her in as they darkened, with red flecks forming around the pupils, a sign that he was just as aroused as she was. She licked her lips, and his eyes dropped to them. He swallowed, trailing his free hand up her arm. Goosebumps formed and a shiver danced down her spine at his gentle touch.

The ever-present voice of reason whispered in the back of her mind, telling her he was only using her, to not fall for those sinful eyes. The other voice, however, had a louder, stronger pull. It told her that he might be a devil—a Lucifer at that—but she was a djinni. She could be just as cunning. She should continue to play the innocent, clueless role to make him think he had control over her.

Slowly, he leaned forward. Anticipation sent her heart racing as she prepared to meet him halfway.

"Remi, did you see that fancy-ass limo that parked out front—"

Remi and Rhys jumped away from each other as her door was thrust open. With burning cheeks, she turned to see Silas and Gracie watching them both with shocked eyes. For several long moments, the four of them stayed like that, Rhys and Remi looking guilty while the two intruders pieced together what they'd just walked in on.

An awkward silence ensued, no one knowing quite what to say.

Then Rhys cleared his throat, turning to her. His expression smoothed over to be cool elegance once more. "I'll be waiting downstairs when you're ready." He nodded to Silas and Gracie and slipped past them, grabbed her two bags of luggage from beside the door and left. Remi's friends were gawking at him all the while.

When they could no longer hear his footsteps clomping down the stairs, they both turned to her, slamming the door shut.

"What in the gods' names did we just interrupt?" Gracie asked, curving her lips into a wide smile. "Holy shit. You two were about to kiss, weren't you?"

"What? No," Remi lied, turning away to retrieve her purse from the bedroom. Her friends followed, of course.

"Lies," Silas said, his dark eyes twinkling with mischief. "Dammit, Grace, I knew we should've walked slower. She could have gotten some action."

"There's no action," Remi groaned, her cheeks on fire as she grabbed her purse. "I was just looking at his hand because Pepper bit him."

"Mm-hmm. And I'm actually a dew fairy who pukes rainbows."

Gracie chuckled. "Don't worry, Silas. They're totally gonna fuck when they get to the hotel."

When Remi remained silent, only staring at her friends guiltily, Gracie's mouth dropped to her chest. "My gods! You already have, haven't you?"

Remi's mouth worked, but no words would come out. She didn't know what to say.

Silas threw his head back and chortled with glee. "This is *huge*. You have to give us details."

Remi shook her head. "No. You guys know I don't kiss and tell." Not that she'd even kissed Rhys. Just everything else.

"Fine, but at least tell us how big he was." Silas held his two forefingers about five inches apart. "This?" He increased the distance inch by inch. When her cheeks grew hot several inches later, he muttered, "Oh, my."

Gracie gasped. "She's blushing." She faced Remi. "You're blushing! You *never* blush. It was that good, huh."

"It was amazing, and that's all I'm saying."

Gracie and Silas groaned in frustration. "Well, how many times have you done it?"

"Just once."

"But you're going to do it again this week, right?" Silas demanded. "You have to. As many times as possible! Make the man fall desperately in love with you."

Remi snorted with humor, placing a hand on her hip. "Don't get too excited over this. We agreed it was just a physical release for both of us—nothing more, nothing less. Furthermore, we aren't even going to be in the same room. It was a one-time deal, and I'm fine with that. So, let it go." She pushed past them and headed for the front of her apartment.

"Mm-hm-m," Silas repeated, still grinning. He looked at Gracie. "A hundred bucks says they get it on by Wednesday night."

Gracie waved that aside. "Nah. I give them until tomorrow night. Did you see the way he's been looking at her?"

"Like a dragon hoarding its gold."

Remi rolled her eyes, though her friends' words excited her. Every last one of her most sensitive areas was begging to be touched by Rhys again. There was no denying that. And that look in his eyes as they'd leaned into each other had told her loud and clear that he wanted another taste of what she had to offer. She just wasn't sure if it was because he was attracted to her or he was just pretending to be to get her to accept the promotion.

But there was no way she was telling Gracie and Silas that. Her two friends would conjure up all types of plots to ensnare their boss, and none of them would be remotely appropriate. "Listen… Thanks for looking after Pepper while I'm gone," she said, changing the subject. She didn't want to keep Rhys waiting any longer than necessary, nor did she want to risk them being late and missing their plane. "Her food is in the pantry, and only feed her twice—once in the morning and once in the evening. If she starts begging for more, do not let those puppy eyes fool you. The vet said she shouldn't eat more than that or she'll be constipated. Make sure to—"

"Yeah, yeah. You don't have to keep telling us," Gracie grumbled, shooing Remi out of the door. "Appointment at the groomers tomorrow at twelve, trip to the park at two each day, walks every four hours, checkup at the vet's Wednesday at eight. And if we need anything, call. We've got this, girl. Go…and don't keep your man waiting."

"He's not my—"

Before she could finish, Silas slammed the door in her face. *Her* door to *her* apartment. With an amused shake of her head, she strolled toward the stairs.

Sex or no sex, she would put those naughty thoughts on the back burner and save them for when she settled into bed for the night. At the moment, she anticipated returning topside to be greeted by the warmth of the sun.

* * * *

The next two hours were spent in relative silence as Rhys made a number of phone calls in the back of the limo. Remi spent her time reading the brochure for Fontainebleau Miami Beach, the uber-luxurious, all-expenses-paid hotel where they were going to be staying for the next week.

Situated on the oceanfront from Collins Avenue, the historically and architecturally affluent hotel is one of the best Miami Beach, Florida has to offer. Stretching over twenty-two acres of land, the hotel offers a wide variety of famous restaurants by award-winning chefs, chic nightlife venues, a two-story spa, tons of pool space and – of course – miles upon miles of a beautiful beach to explore.

Her excitement only mounted with each passing minute. She'd been to plenty of fancy hotels growing up with her family, but she'd been so young that she hadn't cared for the glim and glam of it all. Plus, she and her sister had been prevented from taking advantage of the 'vacations' they'd been forced to go on. Their parents had kept them on a tight leash, not wanting them to run free and risking destroying their esteemed name.

Remi rolled her eyes in remembrance. Her sister was the only one she missed. Good riddance to the rest of them. She'd made her decision to set off on her own and embrace her demon roots, and they'd made theirs to disown her. It should have been sad, and at first, it had been lonely, but she hadn't had a single regret since that day.

Remi knew the exact moment the limo slid through the shimmering gate that separated Sheol from topside. It was like a thousand invisible strings tickling over her skin then a rush of power flooding her veins. Now that she was no longer in Sheol, her natural magic returned to her, filling her body with energy that made her feel as though she could run a marathon. Better yet, she could block her emotions from Rhys and any other demon who'd be able to sense what she was feeling.

She'd forgotten how drained she'd felt upon first crossing the gate. Passing into a world she wasn't born in had stripped her of her powers, but they were back. On the contrary, Rhys and the other demons who'd be attending the conference would feel drained, the lack of demon powers in the human world making them all but mortal.

She glanced at him when he pulled a silver necklace over his head and tucked it under his tie. Instantly, the horns on the top of his head disappeared. "What is that?"

He frowned, patting his hair. "It contains a glamor spell to hide our demon features. We all have to wear one to blend in with the humans." He reached under the seat and handed her a similar one. It was an ordinary silver chain that was as thin as single thread, yet when she touched it, the magic embedded in the metal tingled along her skin. "Even though you have none that I can see, your eyes tend to flash red when you're…excited."

Remi's lips twitched into a smile while she turned away from him to don the necklace. They both knew what he meant by 'excited'. It was a demon thing. Almost everyone's eyes turned a shade of red if they were angry or aroused. And Remi had definitely been aroused since meeting her boss.

Rhys chuckled but didn't comment further. His phone rang and he answered it, giving her time to think. She wanted Rhys. Her friends knew it. She knew it. And Rhys damn sure knew it. The man was far too handsome for his own good, and he oozed sex appeal. Every time he approached her, passion stirred on the spot, and each day it was getting harder to keep it contained.

Yet she had to be careful. It was clear he was trying to use her, but that was fine. She could dance around his devious plot of seduction. Now that she was aware, she could keep reminding herself that he wasn't someone for her to get close to. She could continue to sleep with him without risking heartbreak, and in the end, when he admitted his faults, she'd flash a triumphant grin and reveal that she'd also been using him all along. Two wrongs didn't make a right, but demons weren't really known for their pure hearts.

With a small smile, she studied his profile. She dropped her gaze to the sensual curve of his lips as he spoke to whoever was at the other end of the line. She wondered what they would feel like if they were kissing where she was already soaking wet.

Likely sensing her rush of arousal, Rhys, still on the phone, turned to her. Their eyes met and his pupils expanded. Remi licked her lips, all sorts of naughty thoughts playing in her mind. Holding his attention, she leaned back, leisurely dragging the nails of one hand down her cheek to the top button of her blouse. She toyed with it for a moment before popping it loose.

Rhys gave a hard swallow, his grip on his phone tightening. "Yes, that sounds like a plan," he bit out. He cleared his throat, though he didn't look away from her. "No, no. I'm fine."

Remi moved to the second button, revealing the top of a silky yellow bra. Her smile widened when his lips parted. His excitement further turned her on, emboldening her.

She used both hands to cup her breasts through her blouse. Rhys fumbled with his phone as his eyes widened. "N-no, I'm still here. Uh-huh. I'm listening. Uh-huh…"

Remi slid her hands down her thighs to the hem of her pencil skirt. She wore dark nylon stockings that stopped mid-thigh, and when she uncrossed her legs, she spread them wide to give Rhys a tiny peek of the matching yellow panties.

He drew in a sharp breath, his eyes drooping low. Remi took that as a good sign. She finger-walked her hand until she was able to push the skirt back to give him a better view.

"Parker, I'll call you back," he snapped, his tone low and deep. *Sexy.* He didn't wait for a response from the man on the other line. He hung up and tossed his phone on the seat beside him. He loosened his tie. "You're playing with fire, Remi."

Remi's eyes dropped to his crotch, where the outline of his hard-on was evident. "Maybe I like the heat of the flames," she murmured. She shifted in the seat to where she was able to pull her skirt over her hips. Rhys sucked in another sharp breath.

"Stand too close and you'll regret it," he growled.

"Mm-m." Remi toyed with the line of her panties before sliding a finger underneath the fabric. Her eyes fluttered closed and she bit her lip. "I think I'm wet enough to avoid getting burned, Rhys." She lifted her eyes halfway. "Wanna see?"

"Fuck yeah."

Rhys closed the distance between them, settling on the floor between her legs. He gripped both of her thighs and massaged before pulling them apart. Remi gasped, her heart racing when he leaned forward to inhale the scent of her excitement, then placed his lips to her panties. She bucked at the feel of his tongue pressing the silky fabric into her clit. "Oh," she breathed, sliding her fingers into his soft hair.

Rhys pulled on her legs until he was able to rest them over his shoulders, giving him better access. He skimmed one hand along her inner thigh, teasing her skin until he used his fingers to caress the edge of her underwear. With a quick jerk, he shoved them aside, baring her skin to him.

"You're soaked," he purred with delight, blinking at her. He flashed a wicked grin. "I've been waiting to do this for two weeks." Still holding her gaze, he leaned forward and gave her a long, loving lick.

Remi's body spasmed, but Rhys moved his other hand to her sternum, holding her in place as he continued to lap at her flesh. Each swipe of his tongue on her clit set her panting, and when he shifted his mouth to suck on it, she damn near yanked his hair from his scalp.

"Rhys," she moaned, thankful that the blacked-out window separating them from the driver was soundproof. Rhys hummed into her, the vibration shooting all the way up to the hardened peaks of her nipples.

Rhys teased the opening of her entrance, circling it with a single finger until he was able to slip it inside. Mimicking the actions of a real cock, he stroked in and out while pleasuring her with his tongue.

The sensation was freaking phenomenal. The man was no novice at this. Remi continued to tug at his hair as her breathing grew into short pants of need. Something deep in her pelvis became coiled, growing tighter and tighter. When he slipped a second finger inside and crooked them at an angle that brushed her G-spot, the coil snapped.

"Ah!" Remi cried out as bursts of color exploded behind her eyes, a powerful orgasm tearing through her. Still, Rhys licked and sucked her juices until she was a trembling mass of loose limbs.

With a final lick, he sat back on his heels and peered down at her nude mound. He licked his lips and grinned, looking satisfied, despite his own needs not having been taken care of. "Beautiful," he murmured. "Absolutely beautiful."

Though she'd just had another of the best orgasms of her life, heat once again pooled within her. She was far from sated, and she wanted nothing more than to have Rhys yank his pants down and pound away at her until she came again.

Instead, he smirked and returned to his seat, leaning back with the cool grace he was renowned for. "As fun as this game is, we're approaching the airport. Compose yourself."

Compose myself? Remi thought in bewilderment. *That arrogant…conceited…asshole. Oh, he* is *good.*

For him to sit there and act like he wasn't affected, as if pleasuring women with his mouth was just another common task for him, further made her believe he was just trying to seduce her for his own motives.

The thought almost made her laugh out loud, but she bit the inside of her cheek to refrain. She was *so* diving into his little game, and the more she thought about it, the more amused she became over the shocked look he'd have when he realized she was going to win.

Schooling her expression to be one of cool indifference, she tugged her skirt into place, buttoned her shirt and tucked a stray curl behind her ear. Then, she pulled her phone from her purse and casually scrolled through it as if she were checking messages, humming to herself. She made sure to keep her mental walls in place. No sense risking him finding out her true intentions. To misquote an age-old saying, she was going to take the devil by his horns.

Chapter Eight

Rhys boarded the private jet that would carry them from New York City — one of the many gateways from Sheol to the human world — to Miami Beach, with a quiet Remi following behind him.

Her silence bothered him, though he couldn't say he blamed her. He'd dismissed her back in the limo, purposely pushing her away. Though Remi didn't seem to be at risk of falling for him, it was a natural defense mechanism that he'd grown accustomed to.

He couldn't afford to have any woman falling for him. They were just troublesome, always wanting this, always needing that. They were never satisfied having just a physical relationship. The sex would start out great, no strings attached, no commitments. Both sides would agree to the situation. Then, in a few days, they'd start complaining because 'he's too busy' or 'he's not showing me enough attention' or some shit. It happened every. Single. Time.

Then there was always the dreaded we-need-to-talk, in which he'd have to sit the women down and give them the whole *'It's not you, it's me'* spiel. There were always tears involved, followed by begging, followed by great bursts of anger and lots of name-calling—all directed at him—while he'd sit back and down shots of whiskey to drown out the sound of nagging.

Yeah, he'd pass on going through that shit again. Better keep with one-night-stands and making it clear there would never be anything more between them. He'd only settle down in the next few months when he'd be forced to take a meek wife, and even then, it would just be in name.

Still, as he watched Remi settle in the recliner-style chair on the other side of the aisle, he tried getting a read on her emotions, only to come up to a blank wall. It wasn't the first time she'd been able to block him, but unlike the others, there weren't even the slightest cracks he could dig through. She was completely sealed off from him, something that was far more annoying than it should have been.

On the outside, she looked the same as always—calm and unconcerned, as though his indifference to her didn't bother her in the slightest. He supposed he should be thankful that she was proving to not be clingy.

She retrieved the little booklet for the hotel they'd be staying in, unfolding the brochure to view it once again. "This resort looks beautiful," she said nonchalantly, as if he hadn't just made her scream her release a little while ago. "I've never been there."

He lifted a brow, glancing up from typing on his phone. "You've ventured to the human world before?"

She froze, her hand pausing in the middle of turning a page. Evidently, she hadn't meant to reveal that tidbit of information.

Which was strange, as he thought about it. Only the highest-ranking demons were allowed to leave and enter Sheol. The others who had that type of authority were Thorne's reapers and charons, and that was just because it was their job to do so. Anyone else had to have a special pass from the ruler of their particular realm — in Elysium's case, Damien Lucifer — and even then, it had to be for a damn good reason, along with a *very* large sum of money.

And on a data entry clerk's salary, it would take several decades to accumulate that type of wealth to purchase just one ticket.

Continuing as if she hadn't just uncovered a deep secret, Remi shrugged, though it was a bit forced. "My family planned a trip topside once upon a time."

Rhys narrowed his eyes. It was impossible to tell whether or not she was lying, since her emotions were still blocked to him. But if she was telling the truth, he wondered what the hell her family did to make so much money or to earn a pass into the human world, not just for one of them, but for an entire family trip. The mystery surrounding her continued to grow, and something in him was itching to solve it.

Who are you, Remington Sawyer? He made a mental note to call Kelle and have her do some digging. If she couldn't find anything, he'd get her to hire a PI.

Boisterous laughter broke out from the front of the plane, and both he and Remi peeped to see Thorne board with his highest officers — two men — followed by Quin with three of his own — two women and one man. Introductions were made and Remi greeted them all with an easy smile before settling into a seat with them at the front of the jet. Rhys, Thorne and Quin made their way to the more secluded area in the back. Since everyone's demon senses were dulled by entering the human world, the distance would keep them out of earshot, despite the two groups being able to see each other.

"Well, it seems you two are getting along," Thorne said with a grin, leaning back in his recliner.

Rhys lifted a skeptical brow. "Is there a reason why we shouldn't be?"

Thorne shrugged, signaling for one of the two stewardesses to bring him a drink. "You tell me."

"How's the workload been going since she started filling in for Ivan?" Quin asked, changing the subject.

Rhys shook his head and continued responding to emails on his cell phone. "She finished everything after the fourth day, along with correcting Ivan's nearly setting us all back two decades."

Quin whistled a low tune. "Impressive. Does that mean she's accepting the job offer?"

"Not quite. She's only helping until after this convention and I have time to hire someone else."

"But you still plan on convincing her?"

Rhys scoffed. "Of course. She's the best COO I've had in twenty years, and she's only been doing it for a little over a week. I'd be a fool to not try to convince her."

"Does she want a job in my department? I can use that type of skill under me."

Thorne, ever the immature gutter-mind, snorted. "I'm sure she has all types of skills that could be put to use *under* you."

Quin grunted and Rhys' typing faltered in annoyance at his brother's teasing words. "Do us all a favor and keep your inappropriate jokes to yourself."

"Who said I was joking? She's fucking hot, man." Thorne leaned forward to peer around the seat in front of him. Rhys nearly growled at him for his smile when Remi crossed her legs, the end of her skirt hiking an inch up her thigh. "I would have been scouting the lower level of your division years ago if I'd known someone like *that* was working for you. That body… And look at those goddamned lips…"

Rhys tightened his grip on his phone, the only visible sign of his growing temper. His brother admiring Remi pissed him off, which was just…ridiculous. He wasn't a jealous man. Besides, Remi was just his employee. Granted, he wanted to spend the next several nights fucking her until they both passed out, but she was an employee, nonetheless. He didn't care if every man in Elysium wanted to ogle her.

He didn't. He shouldn't.

"I highly doubt you're her type," Rhys muttered, keeping his tone neutral. "She's classy." *And wicked. And so damn naughty in all the best ways.*

"What *is* her type?" Quin murmured.

That time, Rhys paused, lowering his phone to stare at Quin. His younger brother was looking around the cabin, though more than once his gaze landed and lingered on Remi.

While Rhys had expected that question from Thorne, it shocked him that it had instead come from Quin. As a germaphobe and introvert, he never showed any interest in anyone, even beautiful women who preened for his attention. It could simply be a matter of

Quin being curious or just pushing Rhys' buttons the way Thorne loved doing, but Rhys wasn't so sure.

He studied Quin, then brushed the feeling off as him overthinking. Remi was pretty, sure, but there had been plenty others just as beautiful who'd all but thrown themselves at Quin and had been turned down. His brother was just…uninterested. Remi would be no different.

Thorne, however, was the one he'd have to keep an eye on. His youngest brother would screw anything with a heartbeat and a vagina. He shook his head, continuing with his email. "I haven't the slightest clue, but you're more than welcome to ask her yourself."

Quin only cleared his throat and turned to look out of the window as the jet began to ascend.

The flight was a little over three hours long, but Thorne was knocked out before they fully left the ground. A quick glance to the front told Rhys that the officers were still getting along, Remi chatting it up with the other two females while the men conversed among themselves.

For a moment, she glanced up and their eyes met, and Rhys was reminded of the way she'd moaned as he'd licked and sucked on her. The memory had his body heating, but then she turned away and continued her conversation.

Blinking to clear his thoughts, he retrieved his laptop from his suitcase and reviewed their itinerary. He'd already done so twenty times before leaving, memorizing every word, date, time and address, yet looking over it once again gave him something to focus on other than Remi.

* * * *

Just as the brochure promised, the Fontainebleau Hotel was nothing short of luxurious. As Remi waited in the elegant Chateau lobby while Rhys and his brothers checked the rest of them in, she gazed around in wide-eyed awe at the beautiful interior, while crowds of people passed through to explore the grounds.

The marble flooring was white with black bowtie designs in it, and there were massive golden chandeliers hanging from the ceiling, splashing the lobby with a brilliant rich glow. The Bleau Bar on the far side had its own area under neon blue lights with a pink light shining on the bar. Despite it being just a bit after noon, many people flooded the room, drinking and chatting away, all smiles. There were several doors and entrances leading everywhere, and Remi was sure that if she'd come alone, she would have gotten lost in the great expanse of it all.

Carmen and Maya, the women who'd accompanied Quin, turned to Remi with wide smiles. "Since we essentially have a free day today, what do you ladies say we get some drinks later?"

Remi grinned, more than pleased to have some female companions to balance out the testosterone that she knew would be thick in the air during the convention. "I'd have to check with Rhys first to make sure he doesn't need me to go over anything, but I'm game."

She'd gotten along with the two of them since the start of their flight. They were both relaxed and easy-going, and they always had something interesting to say. There was no senseless gossip or awkward pauses as they struggled to figure out what to say next. They'd treated her as if they'd known her for a lifetime, which made it far easier for her to chat casually with them.

Maya, a panther-shifter with long, glossy black hair and bright blue eyes, snorted. "I'm sure the biggest stick-in-the-mud in all of Elysium would find something for you to do. The man wouldn't know what fun was if it slapped him across that chiseled jaw."

"He is a bit of a workaholic, isn't he?" Remi said with a laugh.

"I'll say," Carmen replied, chuckling. She was the shortest of them, with icy-blonde hair cut into a pixie style. It matched her delicate features. Like Gracie, she was a false angel with wide sea-green eyes that gave her a look of innocent beauty. Also like Gracie, the woman was bold and spoke what was on her mind. "He hasn't had a day off since he took over the company twenty years ago."

Remi's eyebrows shot up. "No kidding. Not even a sick day?"

"Not even one. Not only does he oversee the Soul Distribution Center, but he also handles anything directly dealing with Elysium in the other realms, while Thorne and Quin remain home-based and manage their departments."

Surprise flitted through Remi at that bit of news. "Why don't they help him?"

Maya and Carmen frowned at each other. "Well...they can't." At Remi's confused look, Maya elaborated, "All of Elysium is powered by EUC. Rhys has to not only head soul distribution—the largest branch to work in, by the way— but he's also training to take over his father's position as Elysium's next ruler. That's why he's been away from the company for the last few years. As the eldest Lucifer of his generation, he's the only one who has to deal with whatever goes on inside our realm. All Quin and Thorne can do is manage their own divisions and pick up the pieces every time SDC begins to crumble."

Carmen nodded in agreement. "And believe me, it definitely crumbles. Rhys needs a strong COO to stand in his place and help shoulder his burdens, but those buggers are always running off after a handful of months. I remember one guy left after only two days." She paused, shaking her head. "He's lucky you stepped in and saved his ass these last couple of weeks, Remi, but I don't blame you one bit for only doing this temporarily. Not even I would take that offer, and I've been Quin's COO for ten years now."

Maya nodded, peering at her phone. "And I for seven."

Remi was stunned into silence. She'd known Rhys had a lot on his plate, but she hadn't thought that it went beyond EUC. Training to be the next ruler? Good gods below, no wonder he was desperate to find a decent COO. He had so much to do as it was, that having to break away from it all to try to find a replacement must be stressing the hell out of him. That bit of knowledge made her relieved that she'd offered to help him for a while, if only because it eased some of the pressure he had on his shoulders.

It also made her consider accepting the job full-time, but that was a leap she was still reluctant to agree to. She wanted to help him, but becoming COO was something she was going to have to take a long time to think over before signing her life away. While she was confident in her skills and could work under pressure, at some point she was going to snap. All the other officers had. She didn't think she'd be any different.

Oh well, she thought as she saw the brothers returning from the concierge's desk. She'd dwell on it later, after she got settled into her room. At the moment, she wanted to unpack her bags, relax for the next couple of hours then set out to explore what the Fontainebleau Miami Beach had to offer.

* * * *

Alone with Rhys on one of the upper floors, Remi faltered when she noticed the lack of doors. She glanced around. "Which one is mine?"

Rhys snorted and used his key to unlock one of the large double doors. "We have the Sorrento Penthouse. Five bedrooms, so feel free to choose your own room."

Remi raised her eyebrows as she followed Rhys inside, gasping at the beauty of the room. She didn't know where to begin as she took in the spacious luxury suite. It had two levels, and as she strolled through, she eyed the gray flooring and white walls decorated with beautiful paintings. Far on her left was an open-floor living room set with black leather couches squared off to face a TV that could have taken up her bedroom's entire wall. Adjacent to the living room was a short hall that separated the kitchen and dining room from two bedrooms, one of which contained the master suite. Two sliding glass doors revealed the balcony beyond the living room, offering views of the ocean. A quick glance outside exposed a set of patio furniture under large umbrellas and a mini staircase that led to a private Jacuzzi and pool.

Oh my, how fancy, she thought, taking in the lushness of it all.

Returning to the living room, Rhys watched her with amusement, one corner of his lips hiked into a small smile. "Beautiful, isn't it?"

"It is," she breathed, moving to the stairs. The black steps curved upward and disappeared beyond the upper level. "This place is amazing. But why so much space? I would have been fine with regular rooms. That would be much cheaper, too."

Rhys shook his head and rolled his luggage toward the kitchen. "Cheaper, sure, but not as comfortable. Besides, despite my brothers renting their and their officers' individual rooms, I know them well enough to know they will spend ninety percent of the time here, even crash a few times."

"Nice, nice," Remi muttered, not paying much attention. She was too busy admiring the roomy kitchen — black marble countertops with rich wooden cabinets with Miele appliances. "I'm going to go out on a limb and assume you're taking the master bedroom?"

Rhys said nothing, only gave her a dry look as if to say, *'Is that even a question?'*

Remi chuckled. "Just making sure. I'm going to go choose one upstairs."

She could have sworn she saw a flash of disappointment cross his features, but it was so swift that when she blinked, he was looking his usual all-business self. "Very well." He moved past her to stroll down the hall. Without a backward glance, he said, "We'll unpack and get settled in. Once you're done, we'll go over the itinerary, discuss what to expect from the convention, who you'll be meeting and the basics. Afterward, you're free to do as you please."

Remi rolled her eyes. *There he goes again, being a pompous stick-in-the-mud.* She almost wished she had a crucifix to throw at the back of his head. Of course, it wouldn't do much damage unless it had been blessed by a priest, but a little singeing on his perfect, tight ass would have been rather satisfying. Instead, she sighed, grabbed her luggage and headed upstairs.

Chapter Nine

Having unpacked and rested for a while, Remi sat on one of the couches with her legs folded under her as she and Rhys went over the last page of his annoyingly long to-do list—annoyingly long because it had taken damn near three hours to review it and another hour for him to quiz her, which she'd passed with flying colors, thanks very much. Jeez, the man had planned everything they needed to do with specific times that they were to do them. The only thing missing was his scheduling restroom breaks, and even then, she was afraid to bring it up. He might jot them down for the hell of it.

Five minutes at eleven-fifty a.m. Five minutes at four-fifty p.m. Two minutes at six-forty p.m. to wash hands before dinner.

The thought made her snort with laughter, which in turn had Rhys pausing to narrow his eyes. "Something funny?" he demanded.

"Well, yes, actually—"

The gods must have known she was going to say something sarcastic and piss Rhys off, because she was interrupted by a sharp knock at the door. "I'll get it!" she exclaimed, jumping to cross the floor before he could answer his question. She was relieved to catch a break. *Freaking hell.* She'd memorized everything on his itinerary as well as she knew her own name. He'd wasted her whole day of exploring for his nonsensical schedule. How hard was it to remember to attend the convention, socialize, discuss stats and ideas then return to the penthouse by sundown to regroup? Not freaking hard, if she did say so herself.

She unlocked the latch and swung one of the doors open. Quin Lucifer stood there, the scent of eucalyptus and sanitizer rolling off him. His toffee-colored eyes blinked down at her, and all Remi could do was stare back.

Quin was just as gorgeous as his two brothers. That was a given. Up close, she got to study him better. His eyes were lighter than his brothers' and his lips were fuller, well-defined and made to please a woman. He was also taller than them by a couple of inches and wearing a navy polo shirt tucked into khaki pants. His hair was longer than Rhys' and was finger-combed away from his handsome face, the ends curling just past a strong chin that sported a shadow.

"Hi," he murmured. "May we come in?"

Remi blinked, noticing Thorne was standing behind his large frame, along with Maya, Carmen and one of Thorne's employees... *Bobby, is it?*

"Sorry. Come on in," she said, holding the door open wide. "Make yourselves comfortable."

As the five of them entered and greeted her and Rhys, she shut the door and returned to the living room where everyone had gathered. She took a seat in the corner of an L-shaped couch, right between Maya and Quin.

"Where are Colin and Desmond?" Rhys asked his brothers, referring to the two absent officers.

"Desmond tends to have air sickness and hasn't been feeling well since we landed," Quin said. "I suggested he stay in for the night and rest. I just picked up Maya and Carmen on the way here."

"Colin's been dead to the world from the moment he stepped inside his room," Thorne called from the kitchen. "Pun intended. Bobby and I went down to Bleau Bar for a drink."

Remi gasped, widening her eyes in mock surprise. With a tone dripping pure sarcasm, she said, "Wait a minute. You mean to tell me that neither of you went over your itinerary with your officers for *four* hours? What kind of anarchic monsters are you?"

Rhys glared at her while the others laughed. "Ha-ha. You have never attended a Séance Convention, so it was necessary to discuss every aspect with you before tomorrow."

Thorne smiled at her, flashing gleaming white teeth. *Holy smokes, he could be the spokesman for dental commercials.* "Based on her ability to clear out Ivan's multiple weeks of backed-up paperwork in four days flat, I'm sure she could have glanced over your schedule with ease instead of wasting four fucking hours." He paused, giving an apologetic dip of his head. "Excuse my French, ladies."

Rhys sighed in exasperation, organizing his papers and sticking them in his suitcase. "What the hell are you even doing in the kitchen?" he demanded.

"Looking for— Aha! Here they are." Thorne reached high into one of the upper cabinets and pulled down several wine glasses. He grabbed the two complimentary bottles of champagne that had been sitting in a bucket on the counter, crossed the floor with them and handed everyone a glass. "Let's get this party going."

"That's what I'm talking about," Carmen said, straightening with eagerness. Remi smiled at the way neither she nor Maya nor Bobby seemed to care that their bosses—as well as the highest-ranking demons in Elysium—were in the room with them. It was clear that multiple years of working at the side of the Lucifers had stripped away all traces of professionalism among them. The officers were close to their bosses, having formed a type of kinship that allowed them all to enjoy a casual atmosphere.

Remi wondered if Rhys had ever had a COO who had been like that with him. Hell, did the man have any friends at all outside his brothers?

She doubted it. She felt sorry for him, to have to shoulder all his burdens alone with no one to vent to.

As Thorne went around pouring everyone a glass of the sparkling liquid, Quin crinkled his nose in disgust. "You didn't wash these," he grumbled.

Thorne paused. He brought the glass close to his eyes, inspecting it. "Looks clean to me, brother," he said with a shrug, then proceeded to pour his drink before setting the bottle on the coffee table. "Besides, it's not like we'll catch some kind of human sickness."

Quin remained quiet, only staring into his drink. Remi tilted her head to the side. "Is something wrong?"

Thorne scoffed. "Nah, nothing's wrong with him. He's just a big puss—*oomph*!" He broke off when Bobby elbowed him in the rib. "Uh, sorry again, ladies. I mean, he's a bit germophobic. Don't pay him any mind." He tossed his drink back, grimacing with disgust. "Complimentary wine my ass! This shit is disgusting!"

Remi ignored him and leaned toward Quin. "Is that true?" she whispered.

Instead of answering, he frowned, and the tops of his cheeks turned a bright shade of red. She didn't need to be a devil to see that he was embarrassed by the truth in his brother's words.

She took the glass from his hands and stood, making her way to the kitchen while disregarding the curious eyes on her. She emptied both of their drinks into the sink then ran hot water over them for several moments, making sure every inch of them had been rinsed. Shaking them dry, she returned to the couch and poured more wine into their glasses. She handed one to Quin, who was watching her with shocked eyes.

She smiled at him. "There's no telling how long those glasses have been in the cabinet unattended. I don't blame you one bit for being wary."

Quin gave her a relieved, grateful smile and took a sip from the cleaned glass, still watching her. Aware that everyone was staring at her in amazement — Thorne with his mouth gaping — she raised her glass to them. "We have a long week ahead of us. Didn't someone say something about a party?"

With the awkward moment passing, the others gave a hearty cheer and indulged in conversation. Rhys was more reserved, only speaking here and there, though he looked out of place while the rest of them chatted, laughed and drank for the next hour or so. Remi's gaze kept straying toward him, wanting to comfort him somehow and encourage him to open up. At the same time, however, she didn't want to do so without drawing too much attention, which might make him feel uncomfortable at being put on the spot.

There were a few times when his eyes met hers, and the sexual tension between them would spark to life. She wanted to know what he was thinking, because the steamy looks she was purposely giving him made it clear what was on her mind.

Carmen was the first to notice when both bottles were empty. "Bugger," she grumbled, glancing at Rhys. "Don't suppose they gave you more than these, did they?"

Before he could answer, Thorne jumped to his feet. "Nah, forget that. Let's go down to the bar and get some real drinks instead of this froufrou shit. I don't even have a slight buzz."

Maya giggled and stood, swaying ever so slightly. "Howz about...we swim! Yeah, let's go shwim!" She pressed her palms together and wiggled them, mimicking a fish.

Remi grinned, amused that she'd figured out who the lightweight was out of them all. "Oh gods. Didn't she only have two glasses?"

Carmen rolled her eyes. "One and a half. She's not even finished with her second one."

Bobby chuckled, shaking his head. Despite having a common-ass name, his accent was thick with a Scottish brogue. "Poor lass. Can't even hang with the big dogs."

Maya gasped, looking around in disgust. "Dogs? Ewww, I hate dogs. They make my fur stand on end."

"That's because you're a cat, buttercup."

Maya flipped him off. Well, tried to. Instead, her index finger popped up, though she must not have noticed because she had a smug smile on her face and muttered, "Take that."

Thorne snorted with humor. "So, what's the plan, folks? It's only seven o'clock, and I, for one, have no desire to sit around bored out of my mind when we have a free night to party." He lifted a brow at Maya. "Well, she might not be able to hang much longer."

"Don't underestimate a shifter," Quin chided. "Though they get drunk fast, their metabolism is in high-gear. She'll be sober again in no time."

"Sounds like you know from experience," Remi commented, taking the last sip of her glass.

Quin shrugged. "This isn't her first time enjoying the first night of the Séance Convention. Believe me."

"Yeah," Carmen added, "Quin's seen us drunk plenty of times. Desmond especially."

Thorne cleared his throat, growing impatient. Remi looked around at the others. "I didn't bring a bathing suit to swim."

Thorne winked. "You can always go skinny dipping, love. I'll join you."

Rhys glared at him, but she laughed it off. "Polite pass. I could eat though." She looked at her two female companions. "I read in the brochure there were a few restaurants around here that double as a bar and lounge. Want to go check them out?"

Maya gasped, her glazed eyes widening. "Stripsteak. Oh, my gods, I could go for a steak right now."

Carmen nodded in agreement. "Let's go. I've only had breakfast, so I'm starving."

"We'll come too," Thorne smiled, waving at Bobby to follow him toward the door.

"Are you coming?" Remi asked Rhys and Quin.

"No, thank you. I have emails to respond to," Rhys said, pulling out his laptop. "I'll order room service." While his computer loaded, he brought his phone to his face as if typing a serious message.

Remi fought the urge to roll her eyes. She understood he was busy, but his nonstop acting high-and-mighty was grating on her nerves. Well, in hindsight she supposed he had a right to act that way given his social status in Elysium, but still...

She peered at Quin. "What about you?"

He hesitated. She knew he wanted to join them, but large crowds full of coughing and sneezing must put him on edge. She flashed him a comforting smile. "We'll get a private table, away from everyone else. And I'm sure they'll have prewrapped disposable forks and spoons, as well as to-go cups and plates. You won't have to touch any of the real dishes."

After another moment, he nodded and rose from his seat. Rhys lowered his phone and watched his brother, his expression a mix of shock and confusion. Then he looked at Remi and back at Quin. Narrowing his eyes, he slid his phone into his pants pocket and stood as well. "On second thought, I'll go. Chef Michael Mina's Black Truffle Risotto is to die for."

"You can just order that in room service," Thorne drawled, though his eyes held a knowing twinkle.

"Shut it," Rhys growled, moving to the head of the group as they filed out the penthouse.

Remi just watched him with curiosity, wondering what was up with his sudden change of heart. Then she peered up at Quin, a sudden thought occurring.

Is he jealous?

Remi couldn't stop the mischievous smile curling one corner of her lips. Perhaps he was worried that she'd grow attracted to his brother, thus ruining his plans to seduce her into becoming COO.

Oh well, there's only one way to find out.

* * * *

Remi was up to something. Rhys could feel it in his bones. Every time he glanced at her across the table, she had a little smirk on her face that he was sure had nothing at all to do with the conversation.

Then again, it could be a result of paranoia creeping in from his endless burdens. Perhaps the stress of it all was catching up to him, throwing him off his game and making his mind see things that weren't there.

He blamed it on his dulled senses from being topside. That was the only explanation for why he couldn't sense any of her emotions when she'd been far more open to him the whole time he'd known her in Elysium. Or maybe she'd found a way to block herself.

There goes my paranoia again. There was no way she could manage such a thing. No one could hide their emotions from a powerful devil, even if he didn't have his full senses. And the necklaces they were wearing only hid their demon features, not hindering anything else.

So, what on earth is going on?

And why the hell did I even agree to come to eat with them?

He hadn't lied about having work to do. Plus, he hated public places in the human world. Even elegant ones like Stripsteak were a nuisance to him. Humans were noisy, messy and each of them smelled like a slow death. Yet here he was on one side of the rectangular table stuck between a borderline alcoholic false angel and a rambunctious kelpie whose Scottish accent was growing thicker by the minute. The two were going back and forth like drunken sailors, gulping down drinks to see who could handle more.

Right across from him sat Remi, with Maya on her left and Thorne at the corner. The two had been openly flirting for the past two hours, though such was the norm with them. Though Thorne had a reputation for fucking EUC's employees, even he had a line he wouldn't cross, which was screwing one of the higher officers that he considered a friend. Likewise, the feeling was mutual with Maya, though they still put on a show to entertain themselves, if no one else.

Quin sat at the other end of the table, looking far more comfortable in a public restaurant than Rhys had ever seen him. Plenty of things his younger brother had done had shocked him, and every last one of them had involved Remi in some type of way. Quin never ventured to public places just for the hell of it, and he'd stopped showing interest in women three years ago. Hell, Rhys had thought his brother had preferred the opposite gender once upon a time.

Not that he cared who or what his brother chose to date. So long as the man was happy, all was well. Still, Quin was as straight as they came, but his phobia had pushed him to abstain from all forms of physical contact. If he had to so much as shake someone's hand, he'd go into a full-blown panic if he didn't wash or sanitize immediately afterward.

So yeah, Quin's slight change in behavior had piqued Rhys' interest—his interest *and* his jealousy. Funny how he'd been so adamant that he'd never be jealous over a woman just hours ago, yet there he was, forced into an atmosphere he hated because he hated the sight of Quin's interest in Remi even more.

But that didn't mean anything was going to change. He still was going to keep Remi at an emotional distance and treat her like an employee, for both of their sakes. His petty jealousy was just a passing phase. He'd be over it in no time. Remi certainly seemed to have moved on from him as she laughed at something Quin said.

Yeah, because he's so funny, Rhys thought in annoyance. He downed the rest of his drink, the burn of the alcohol welcome as it warmed him.

"Who's funny?" Bobby asked him, his words slurred from imbibing too much.

Rhys blinked, realizing he'd voiced his sarcastic thoughts. "What are you talking about?" he countered, hiding his embarrassment.

Bobby frowned, squinting his eyes to see better. "I thought you said... Never mind. Bugger, I'm fucked up."

"Ha! I win," Carmen chirped, her own words slurred. Several heads from the nearby tables turned to peer at the sudden outburst. She glared at Rhys, placing her finger to her lips. "Sh-h-h! You're being too — *hiccup* — loud."

Rhys rolled his eyes, signaling for the waitress to bring him the check before his tablemates decided to trash the place. That was just what he needed — a bunch of drunk, rowdy demons drawing the unwanted attention of humans. He glanced at Remi as she finished the last bite of her dessert. "This was the best meal I've had in years," she said with a contented sigh. She smiled at Rhys. "Well, other than when you took me to Marino Cucina. Now *that* was delicious."

Rhys straightened his shoulders and half-smiled. "I knew you'd like it. It's the best Italian restaurant in Elysium."

"Wait! You went to Marino's without us?" Thorne whined, a hurt look passing over his features. "That's so messed up, dude. You know that's my favorite."

Rhys grunted. "It was late in the evening and the first day she agreed to stand in for Ivan. You'd already left by then, probably to intrude into someone's bed."

Thorne snickered. "Oh, right."

Everyone continued with their chatter. Quin shook his head, smiling down at Remi. "How was the dessert? Good, I hope."

Remi tilted her head and smiled sweetly. "Fantastic. Thanks for recommending it to me. I'm going to have to make sure I order at least one more before we leave Miami Beach." She scooped up a bit of fallen whipped icing with her fingertip. With deliberate slowness as if to seduce them—at least that was how Rhys saw it— she slid her finger into her mouth to taste it.

Rhys' throat went dry and his cock swelled as white-hot lust shot through him. Her tongue darted out to catch the tiny dollop that had lingered on her lower lip. He wasn't the only one affected as he took in Quin's lowered gaze.

And damn Canaan's gods to hell if he didn't want to drag Remi away from his brother, shove her against the wall of the closest dark corner and fuck her brains out for making him feel that way. Reputation be damned, he wanted her so bad that the need was driving him insane.

It was the alcohol. It had to be. That was the only explanation. That, and his ever-present stress from his responsibilities. He had to get his shit together and under control, because if the heads of their sister corporations caught on to this weakness, especially those damnable Belials, they were going to send his ass through the shredder — then some.

Chapter Ten

Remi awoke bright and early the next morning, despite having drank the previous night until her vision had blurred. Had she indulged so much in Sheol, she would have a splitting headache from a massive hangover, but as it was, the magic running through her veins gave her extra boosts of energy.

After dinner, they'd all hung out at Bleau Bar for another couple of hours until midnight had hit, but it had been Rhys' grumbled suggestion that they return to their rooms to get some rest before the convention. And speaking of the handsome devil, Remi had caught him sneaking glances at her every time she laughed at something Quin had said — or his brother had laughed at something she'd said.

It had been amusing, but in truth, Quin really was interesting. He was the quieter of the bunch, but when he spoke, he was sweet and funny, and his insecurity over his phobia made him far too adorable for Remi not to try to cheer him up. Likewise, he'd seemed interested in getting to know her, though she was sure it was his way of showing gratitude for her being the only one to not tease him.

Remi laid out her clothes for the day — a black blazer over a white blouse tucked into black straight-leg pants and dark suede pumps. It was nothing too fancy, since today was pretty much all about introductions, where each head of the companies would present PowerPoint slides to show how their individual companies had changed since last year's convention. Given the fact that there were fifteen leaders that would need to take a turn, Rhys had informed her that it would take up the entire day, especially once the Dagons from the Center of Eternal Punishment took the stage. Where Rhys, Thorne and Quin represented Elysium Underworld Corp as its three leaders, CEP had seven of them, each one a symbol for one of the deadly sins, and they always took the longest to announce themselves.

Armano more so, being the Dagon of pride.

With a snort, Remi strolled to the spacious bathroom, where she then ran the water for her shower. Once it was set to her preferred temperature, she peeled her clothes off and stepped under the steamy spray, sighing with delight as the water struck her skin. She stood there for several minutes, just enjoying the shower warming her body before she lathered her loofah.

A half-hour later, Remi's skin was scrubbed pink and her fingertips were wrinkled. She wrapped her body in a fluffy white towel that fell below her knees and her thick hair in a smaller one. She peeked out of the door to make sure the coast was clear, then darted across the hall to close herself into her bedroom. Knowing Rhys, he'd probably slept for about three hours before waking up to start his day, even though they didn't have to be in the convention room until noon.

She chuckled at the thought. He was always so wound up that she wondered if he ever just…relaxed. Even when they had been sitting around drinking and talking to each other, he'd spent the majority of his time on his phone, sending out text messages or emails or whatever the hell he did. One would think Earth would explode if he went one day without touching the cellular device.

After donning her clothes, she returned to the bathroom carrying two small bags — one containing her makeup and the other hair products. She went to work blow-drying her hair, brushing the curls until they were loose and bouncy down her back, then she worked to pull the long strands into a French braid. Once finished, she rolled the braid into a bun and pinned it into place. Then, with a bit of mascara to her lashes and a smidge of red color to her lips, she was ready to go.

She glanced at her wristwatch. Well, she still had three and a half hours. She thought about what she could do until then. Perhaps she and Rhys could get some breakfast and do a bit of exploring.

Better yet, she could go shopping for a bathing suit. She hadn't gone swimming in years, so she hadn't had one to pack, but since her newfound friends wanted to take a dip in the private pool, she could get one to join the fun.

Smiling, she grabbed her purse, checked to make sure her cell phone and wallet were inside, then headed downstairs to Rhys' room. She knocked on the door six times. No response. She knocked six more times. "Hey, bossman, are you awake?" Just for the hell of it, she knocked six more times. Three reps of six. It was fitting. "Rhys, I'm going to get some breakfast. Do you want anything?" She pressed her ear to the cold wood, listening for several moments. Rhys let out a loud snore, his breathing steady.

She clucked her tongue and stepped back, shocked that he was still asleep. Maybe he'd drunk more than his share of alcohol the night before and was sleeping it off. That, and the fact that he was drained from entering the human world, must have worn him out. If that were the case, she didn't want to interrupt his much-needed rest.

She approached the kitchen and scribbled a short note for him, then grabbed a spare keycard and left. The elevator carried her all the way down to the lobby, stopping a few times to allow a handful of people on. She exited and had only taken a few steps forward when she paused, realizing that she didn't have the slightest clue where to go from there. The Fontainebleau was so huge that she could lose ten pounds in one day by walking from one end to the other. And with the number of restaurants, lounges, shops and the gods knew what else, it was hard to remember which way to go.

"Excuse me, ma'am. Are you lost?" a deep, British voice asked from behind her.

She turned to gaze up at a man who was almost the same size as Rhys. He was also dressed in a fine-tailored suit, but the similarities ended there. He was fair-skinned and had a head full of snowy white hair, styled away from his lean, handsome face. His eyes were a stunning shade of blue she'd never seen before, as if a clear spring sky had been swallowed and morphed into two small orbs. His pupils were so tiny that they may as well have been nonexistent, making the irises look even more captivating.

Mesmerizing.

Dangerous.

"Afraid so," she murmured, keeping her tone steady. Though he looked human enough, there was a certain pulse of raw power beneath the skin that told her otherwise. And if her ability to sense another demon's presence wasn't convincing, his perfect smile revealed canines that were a tad bit longer and sharper than normal, which was a dead giveaway that he was an upir.

Or, as the modern-day humans call them, vampires. Well, a form of vampire, as they were quite different from the ones in folklore. "I'm trying to find a good place to get some breakfast."

His smile widened, humor twinkling in his striking eyes. "I'm seeking to get a bite myself."

Remi sized him up, knowing full well what he meant by 'bite'. She shook the urge to cover her neck. "Where do you suggest?"

"Vida has a traditional continental breakfast until eleven. I was just on my way there, if you're interested in joining me."

Remi cocked a brow, scanning his physique from his bare neck to his left ring finger for a sign of a mating mark. "Surely someone with your looks would have a wife or girlfriend eager to dine with you."

He smirked. "I'll take that as a compliment, but no, I do not have anything of the sort. Just haven't found the right one, I suppose." He nodded at her bare hands. "And you?"

"Unattached, at the moment," she murmured. *Unattached, but dying to feel a certain man's touch again.*

"Well, how about that," he announced. He held his arm out to her. "Would you care to join me for breakfast?"

Remi pursed her lips in thought. "We've known each other for five minutes, yet you're already asking me out? That's mighty bold of you."

He winked at her. "I hear it only takes five minutes for a woman to decide whether or not she's interested. Besides, we'll be attending the same conference in a few hours, so we might as well get to know one another beforehand."

Remi knew she shouldn't be surprised, but she couldn't stop herself from stiffening. Upirs had to survive on blood, so their senses were able to differentiate all the creatures they came across. Remi only hoped his senses were too dull for him to figure out exactly what she was.

"True enough," she muttered, still wary. What was the harm in eating breakfast? And hey, if he was paying, that was just a bonus.

Still, she was aware he had some kind of ulterior motive. This wasn't just a chance encounter. Her djinni senses allowed her to see that he was desperate for something, yet it was too blurry for her to figure it out. It made her curious.

"What do you say?" he prompted, his alluring eyes attempting to draw her in. There was something sneaky about him, but she couldn't quite put her finger on it. Her insides were screaming at her to walk as far away from him as she could, but a tiny part of her wanted to find out what secrets he was hiding, and why he'd 'unexpectedly' run into her. She had a good intuition about people, so she trusted her gut feeling that nothing this man did was coincidental.

She pressed her lips into a kind smile. "So long as I'm off the menu, sure."

He chuckled at that. "I'm Graham Belial."

"Remi Sawyer." She slid her hand into the crook of his elbow. He squeezed, allowing her to feel the solid muscle beneath. Then, he led the way.

While he made small talk, Remi pretended not to be disturbed by his name or the feeling of unease sliding through her by touching him.

The Belials and the Lucifers were age-old sworn enemies. In recent decades, they'd put aside their hostility, though it was clear that the two families despised one another. Rhys had made it clear that should a Belial approach her, she should always remain on guard and to not trust them, no matter how polite or charming they appeared. They were conniving liars who could charm the scales off a dragon if they wanted to, she'd been told. It was no secret that they wanted to take over Elysium as their own, and the other officers had warned her that several of EUC's past employees had been persuaded into turning against them to join Bell Towers.

And since she was the only one of the Lucifers' workers who was a newbie, she had been reminded over and over yesterday to never allow a Belial to get her alone, most of all the CEO of Bell Towers—Graham Belial.

Rhys is going to kill me.

* * * *

Rhys awoke with a start, his eyes flying open on a gasp. Blinking several times to clear the haze, he frowned as he tried to figure what the hell had startled him awake. He didn't dream anymore, so it couldn't have been a nightmare. Besides, he was a freaking Lucifer, a descendant of a long line of devils who'd spent millennia scaring the daylights out of mortals. He *was* the nightmare.

A loud pounding sounded again, almost making him jump out of his skin. "What the fuck," he breathed, placing a hand over his thrashing heart.

"Rhys, open up, man!" someone shouted. Was that Quin or Thorne? It was hard to tell from the thick walls muffling the voice.

Grumbling to himself, he didn't bother throwing on a robe, instead opting for stumbling to his room door in only his boxer briefs. He knocked into the wall twice, cursing each time. His head throbbed and his vision was still a bit blurred. Damn, he regretted drinking as much as he had. Sheolic drinks were far stronger than human alcohol, but being topside weakened his resolve, making his tolerance far lower than it should have been.

Stumbling into the main entrance of the penthouse, he growled when whichever brother pounded on the door again, the sound seeming to echo in his head. "Shut up," he snarled, snatching the door open. He glared daggers at Quin. "What?"

Quin parted his lips as he took in Rhys' crabby appearance. "Dude, you look awful. What the hell are you still doing in bed?"

Rhys narrowed his eyes further, mostly in an attempt to focus his vision. "What the devil do you think? I was sleeping."

"This late? Are you hungover?"

Rhys closed his eyes, nausea threatening to send him heaving onto the floor. "What... What are you talking about?"

Quin angled his wrist to show Rhys the time on his watch. It took several moments, but when the knowledge settled in, Rhys gasped. "Eleven-twenty? Shit." He straightened, moving away from the door to return to his room. He paused when he spotted a notepad sitting on the wet bar separating the kitchen from the dining room.

Went to get breakfast. See you at the convention.
P.S. Try using nasal strips before going to bed. Your snoring is a thing of nightmares.
Remi

With a little smiley face and her phone number at the end in case he needed to call her. Rhys' panic was replaced with humor. He wasn't usually a snorer, but he'd crashed the moment he'd crawled into bed the previous night, far too tired from a combination of overdrinking, crossing into the human world and his usual stress.

He shook his head, dropped the note on the counter then proceeded to his room. "I'm going to take a quick shower and get dressed," he told Quin, his sour mood lightening a bit. Remi tended to have that effect on him, it seemed, even when she wasn't nearby.

"I'm about to head down now," Quin called. "You weren't answering your phone, so I figured I'd come to make sure you didn't oversleep."

Yeah, too late for that, Rhys thought wryly. He threw his hand up in a dismissive wave. "Thanks, brother. I'll send a text when I'm on the way down."

He was already in his room when the front door opened and closed. Not wanting to waste any more time, he hopped in the shower and turned it on, flinching when icy pricks of cold water splashed on him before warming. *Oh well.* The shock helped him to clear his mind and shake off the nausea. It took only ten minutes for him to get clean then another fifteen before he was fully dressed, combed and speed-walking out of the door.

He checked his phone and saw that he had twenty-three missed calls, most of them from his brothers. While on the way toward the elevator, he called the most important one...Kelle. His assistant answered on the third ring. "Elysium Underworld Corporation, Rhys Lucifer's office. This is Kelleesa speaking."

"Good afternoon, Kelle."

"Hey, Rhys," she said, her tone reverting to the ordinary casual one she used to speak to him. She was one of the few allowed to do so, though most times she settled for calling him Mr. Lucifer. "I was calling to let you know that I contacted Dietrich's Investigation Services. They're a rather small, independent group on the outskirts of the city, but they're the best Elysium has to offer. Gunter Dietrich runs the place, and he's agreed to perform this task for you in exchange for one free pass topside."

Rhys entered the elevator, grateful that it was empty. He rolled his eyes. "Absolutely not. What kind of ridiculous request is that? Surely his services don't cost half as much sen as it does a trip up here."

Kelle grunted. "No, but you might change your mind after this. Remi isn't from Elysium."

Rhys paused, stepping to the far corner when the elevator stopped to allow three humans onboard. He lowered his voice. "What do you mean she isn't from there?"

"I mean the Remington Sawyer we have on file does not exist anywhere in Elysium. I've done a thorough background check on her, and Sawyer is far too common a name on Boogle for me to find anything solid. Even her Fangsbook social media page is private, though the bit of information there only dates back three and a half years. However, she wasn't born in any of our hospitals, and her birthday on her employee file isn't showing up in any of the older archives. She simply doesn't exist beyond the three years she's been working for us. She wasn't *born* in Elysium."

Rhys' frown deepened, confusion swamping him. In Sheol, it was far easier for demons to travel between the four regions, but it was still a process one needed to go through, just like it was a process for humans to travel to different countries topside. Everything and everyone was documented. However, it wasn't uncommon for demons to live in a region outside the one they were born in. For most, they would become incredibly 'homesick' after being away for too long, with extra emphasis on the being sick part. It became a physical ailment that could only be fixed if they returned to their homeland.

For Remi to not have been born in Elysium, yet working every day for the last three years, that was just…unheard of. That, along with her strange ability to block him and her astonishing capacity to remain cool and complete several weeks' worth of worth in just four days… It was all very suspicious, the more he thought about it.

"Rhys, are you still there?"

Rhys blinked, stepping out of the elevator into the lobby. "Yes, Kelle. I'm here. Tell Dietrich we have a deal and give him my personal email. I want him to notify me the moment he learns something." He and Kelle disconnected, then he made his way through the winding maze of guests toward the events and activities hall.

It took longer than he would have liked, given the number of mortals he had to weave his way through, but he let out a relieved, albeit annoyed sigh when he cleared the way to the conference center. There were several floors containing different-sized rooms for all types of meetings, but Sheol's Séance Convention was held in the space called Glimmer, located on the fourth floor. Every day from noon to five it would be sealed off from all prying human eyes to provide them with total privacy.

Rhys stepped through the opened double doors, his expression its usual professional mask. Since it was almost twelve, nearly all forty-plus guests were already in attendance. He wrote his name on the sign-in sheet lying on a table at the entrance, then made his way inside. Fifty chairs were lined into rows, all facing a small stage with a podium in the center. Wires were hooked up to a laptop and a projector shone a light on the large screen at the back of the stage.

On the far side, where a wall should have been, there were several glass doors leading to the terrace outside, although thick beige drapes were pulled to cover them to keep the room dark enough to allow the projector to shine brighter, as well as provide shelter for the demons who were sensitive to the sun, which was most of them.

Several people were already in their assigned seats, including Rhys' brothers and their officers. But no Remi.

Rhys frowned as he looked around, wondering if she'd gotten lost or was just running behind schedule. She was notorious for being late, of course, but as much as he'd stressed that she needed to be there on time, he was disappointed.

He was about to dial the number she'd left for him when a light, easy laugh drew his attention. He knew that laugh. Turning, he glanced at the door to see Remi round the corner, chatting it up with a human dressed in the hotel's service uniform. "Thank you so much for helping me," she said to the woman, shaking her hand. "I would have wound up near the airport if you hadn't."

Relief filled him even as he pressed his lips together in a stern line. He crossed his arms, signaling his watch when she peeped at him. "Good morn — "

"You're late," he reprimanded.

" — ing." She lifted a slim brow, glancing at her own watch. With a tone sweet enough to give him a cavity, she said, "Oh, my. I'm sorry that I've arrived *exactly* five minutes before the time you told me to be here. Please forgive me for my insolence, Your Majesty."

Rhys' expression didn't change, but he fought to keep from smiling at her sarcasm. She was such a smart-ass, but the way she wasn't afraid to talk back to him or refuse to kiss his ass made it easy for him to relax around her. She was so different from any woman he'd ever met, and while he was still reluctant to get close to her, he couldn't help but think of her as a friend.

Well, perhaps that was a bit of a stretch. They were more like casual acquaintances, Remi someone he could discuss business with in a soothing atmosphere, as well as hump away his stress at the end of the day.

Remi bent over the table to sign her name on the paper. Rhys swallowed a groan and tried not to stare at her ass pressing tight against her dress pants. He remembered all too well having her in that very position just a little over a week before.

When she straightened, he waved toward the middle row where his brothers sat, two empty chairs between Thorne and Quin. The lights flicked on and off, signaling for everyone to take a seat so the convention could start. The doors closed, sealing off all humans from entering.

The two of them moved to take their seats, and Rhys hesitated between deciding which chair to take. Should he sit by Quin, Remi would be next to Thorne, who flirted with anything with a pretty smile—and Remi had a gorgeous smile. On the other hand, if he sat next to Thorne, she'd have to sit by Quin, who was growing an interest in her. Something that bothered Rhys far more than it should have.

He *eeny-meeny-miny-moed* it and sat next to Quin. Hell, Thorne might flirt with Remi, but he knew him well enough to know he wouldn't attempt to fuck her, not when she'd so easily become a part of their inner circle. With Quin, however, there was no telling. In just one day he'd done so many things out of character that proved he had a thing for Remi. The last thing Rhys wanted was to see Quin and Remi become an item. The thought was just…wrong.

It was ironic, given the circumstances, and unfair to both of them. He had no interest in becoming emotionally involved with Remi, yet the thought of her indulging in such with another man, least of all one of his brothers, struck something deep in his heart.

And, yep, he was done analyzing this shit. It would lead to nothing but trouble.

"Nice of you to finally join us," Thorne murmured.

"I overslept."

His brother made a shocked sound in his throat. "*You* overslept? The king of being on time? The one who attends the party three hours early? Say it ain't so."

Remi chuckled, looking straight ahead as she spoke. "It would appear someone else isn't quite the drinker, after all."

"Yes, I am," Rhys grumbled. "The drink I ordered was stronger than yours."

Carmen peeked around Quin's large frame at Remi. "Didn't you have the same drink as him, Remi?"

"Stinger with extra shots of cognac? Yep."

"Okay, but—" Rhys said, only to be interrupted.

"Didn't you drink more than Rhys?" Carmen asked.

"Yep, six to his four," Remi crooned.

"Okay, but—" Rhys started, only to be interrupted by Carmen again.

"Did you oversleep, Remi?"

"Nope. I woke up at seven on the dot."

"All right, dammit," Rhys growled, eliciting laughter from his seatmates. "I overslept. It happens. Now be quiet. The convention is starting."

Chapter Eleven

At last, the PowerPoint slides and introductions were over. For the next hour, Rhys was approached by several members from their sister organizations in The Meadows and Asphodel. He already knew the heads and most of their managers, having met them years before when he'd first taken over his company. There were a few new faces, however, and he introduced himself, though he knew he wouldn't remember their names by the next day. Such was the norm. People came and went, only a handful of workers being loyal enough to stay by the CEOs' sides for more than a year or two.

Quin and Thorne both had theirs. Carmen, Maya, Desmond, Bobby and Colin had worked for his brothers for seven to fifteen years, which explained the closeness between them all. Rhys was the odd one out and everyone knew it, even people from the other corporations. None of his COOs ever stayed long. He'd even spent a few years allowing more than one officer at a time to split the workload, but that had ended in disaster, including a front-row seat in Hades' court, something he'd give his left nut to avoid in the future.

He glanced across the room to where Remi stood near the refreshments table, pouring herself a glass of punch. Two men and two women were around her, laughing at something she'd said. *Figures.* Her presence could captivate an entire audience. Her wit, her charm, her humor... She was a woman people wanted to be around. She just had that type of pull.

"Beautiful, don't you think?" A deep voice announced from beside him.

Rhys steeled his expression, turning cold eyes on his lifelong nemesis, Graham Belial. As was his trademark, the man had an arrogant smile that matched the smug, knowing look dancing in his creepy-ass eyes. "The venue? Absolutely. As always, Shanice did an excellent job setting everything up."

Graham's lips twitched in amusement, because they both knew full well he didn't mean the damn venue with his sarcastic question. "You had a different officer last year. Tierre, I believe was his name. Or was it Cleveland? They come and go so often that I tend to forget."

Rhys didn't bat an eye at the obvious bait. Graham had a knack for trying to get under his skin, and he had long ago learned to ignore the taunts. Instead, he gave an easy shrug. "Not everyone is able to simply laze about like your people at Bell Towers. COO under the Soul Distribution Center is the hardest in all four regions. Very few have the skin needed to take it on."

"Does she?" Graham nodded his head toward Remi. "From what I hear, she's only been with you for a couple of weeks. How much longer before she caves in?"

Rhys took a long sip of his punch, annoyed that he was unable to read his enemy. Graham was close to his age, and as the eldest Belial, he was powerful enough to block out the powers of a Lucifer, even if they both were topside. "Who's to say? People come and go. Could be weeks, could be months." Or she could be the one to prove she could handle the job and remain his COO. If only he could convince her.

Graham chuckled as if he could read Rhys' mind. Which he couldn't, thank the gods. The man would destroy him and pounce on his weakness the first chance he got. And each passing day showed Rhys that Remi was very much becoming his weakness.

"How's the hunt for a wife going?" Graham asked, changing the subject.

Rhys narrowed his eyes. Since Asphodel and The Meadows were both extended lands from Elysium — though they'd gained their own names and leaders — the first-born-must-mate-by-their-hundredth-birthday rule only applied to the Lucifers and the Belials. "Just fine. And you?"

Graham's lips twitched into a cocky smile. "Much the same as yours. Although" — he deliberately trailed his gaze in Remi's direction — "I must say I've found one or two who have managed to garner my interest. Admittedly, I've always had a thing for redheads."

Rhys couldn't help the way his spine stiffened. He clenched his hand around the stem of his glass until it damn near cracked beneath the pressure. Forcing his tone to be steady, he relaxed his shoulders. "If my COO has piqued your interest, you're wasting your time."

Graham lifted a brow that was several shades darker than his hair. "Oh? Is she mated? I don't see a mark on her. Wait! Don't tell me *you* have a thing for her instead?" His tone told Rhys that he knew full well the answer to that question, despite Rhys' attempts to hide it.

"Don't be ridiculous," he countered. "She doesn't belong to any royal family, nor does she have a high-level name in Sheol."

Graham shrugged, sipping his drink while staring over the rim at Remi. There was a knowing twinkle in his eyes that made Rhys suspicious. "I care nothing for politics. My father and forefathers may have been all for taking a wife for namesake only, but I believe it's high time for a change."

Rhys gritted his teeth. He clenched his free hand into a fist that he shoved inside his pocket to keep from choking the other male. "Your father would never allow it."

Graham turned to face Rhys, his playful expression transforming to cold, revealing the true demon hiding behind the arrogant façade. He lowered his voice and stepped close to Rhys. "When I take over Abyssia's throne, my father becomes nothing more than a blip in demon history. I will live by my own rules and do what *I* want, including taking a wife *I* choose. She could be born from rags, for all I care, so long as she pleases me. Unlike you, I know full well when I meet a one-of-a-kind woman. And if you have no desire to take the lovely Miss Sawyer, then I will. That's on my oath."

With that, he roughly patted Rhys on the back and strolled away, heading for the exit. His COOs, two of his cousins who shared his fair looks, followed behind him.

Rhys just stared straight ahead of him, his eyes wide while several emotions rolled through him—anger, frustration, concern, confusion and jealousy, a deep-seated, jade-green monster with a big ugly head that refused to back away. His gaze darted across the room to where Remi was still laughing with the others, oblivious to the fact that he and Graham had just had an entire conversation about her.

A conversation that still had his blood boiling. If he had been jealous over Quin flirting with Remi, the thought of Graham getting near her enraged him, making him want to rip the other man to shreds.

Gods above and below... Why did it have to be her? Why was he feeling these things over *her*? Why not anyone else to be tied down to when he took over as ruler of Elysium? Why couldn't it be any of those damn faceless women his father had waiting in line for him to select from? Why the fuck did it have to be Remi, someone he hardly knew anything about and yet craved in every single way? He wanted to push her away and forget she existed, yet each day that passed he wanted to screw her brains out then hold her and bare his teeth at any man who dared to glance her way.

Why was this happening to him, now of all times? Why when he had to take a mate in a few months and sign his life away to someone he'd never love? Why couldn't he have met her in his adolescent days, when he didn't have a single care over such things as running EUC or taking over Elysium and finding a worthy mate to stand at his side? He could have fallen for her and fucked her as often as he'd liked until he got her out of his system, yet there was no time.

Because every time he looked Remi in her beautiful, ever-changing eyes, he sank farther and farther. There was no way he could break away from her within the next four months. It was a downhill battle, and for the first time in his life, he was losing.

* * * *

Despite sharing the large penthouse suite with Rhys, Remi hadn't seen much of him since Monday. It was Wednesday. The third day of the convention had come to an end, so she'd returned to her private room. She'd only seen him during the last two days, sitting next to him in the meetings. However, he hadn't said much to her.

When he had, it had been monotone and cold, as if he hadn't wanted to be bothered. Whenever they'd return to the suite, he'd go straight to his room and refuse to come out. When she invited him to go out to dinner and the lounges with his brothers and their COOs, he'd decline with some lame excuse about work.

Remi was beginning to think she'd done something to upset him, but she couldn't for the life of her figure out what it was. She'd joked with him like always, but she couldn't remember ever saying anything out of line.

What was more, she was beginning to rethink that he even wanted to seduce her into becoming his COO. Maybe he had just needed to get off to relieve some stress and she had been the closest thing available. They'd agreed on a physical relationship at the start, yet somehow the thought that she was just an outlet for him cut her deep. Even if there were no feelings involved, him seeing her as nothing more than a tool for masturbation was...hurtful.

She froze in the middle of brushing her hair. Could it be that he'd found out she'd eaten breakfast with Graham Belial the first morning? No one had brought it up since then, but could he have known? Was that why he was angry and avoiding her? *Of course!* Graham was her boss' sworn enemy, and she'd known that, yet she'd still had breakfast with him one-on-one. That had to be it.

Dammit, she had to go apologize. The suspense was killing her, and the more she worried over whether or not the man who'd given her the best orgasms of her life hated her, the more her stomach tightened with guilt and stress.

After tossing her brush to the side, she tugged on the thick terrycloth robe that had come with the bathroom towels. She had her new bathing suit on underneath, a one-piece black strip of stretchiness that exposed her back and showed far more cleavage than it covered. It was meant to be sexy and enticing, which was why she'd chosen it when she'd gone shopping the first day. She wanted Rhys to not be able to take his eyes off her, and tonight was the perfect time to show it off. Thorne, Quin and the others were all coming over to take a dip in the private pool and jacuzzi on the patio.

Padding downstairs on the balls of her feet, she made her way to Rhys' bedroom. She listened for a moment before knocking loud enough for him to hear. "Rhys, are you there? Can we talk?" She was met with silence. With a deep, withdrawn sigh, she turned away to head to the living room to watch TV until—

Knock, knock, knock, knock.

Well, hell. She did an about-face and walked to the front door. She pulled it open to see Quin standing there, dressed in a crisp white T-shirt and a pair of blue swimming trunks, with a towel hanging around his neck. She smiled at him, looking past his broad shoulders. "Where's everyone else?"

She stepped aside to allow him to enter. As expected, he smelled clean, like eucalyptus and sanitizer. She wondered just how deep his germaphobia went and how it'd originated. However, she'd never ask him unless he brought it up first. She feared doing so would offend or embarrass him.

"They'll be here eventually," he said to her. "Last I checked, the ladies were fighting over who had the best-looking bathing suit, and Desmond was going to go…um…feed."

Remi hid a smile at the uncomfortable way he stumbled over that word. She'd learned that his third COO was an upir like Graham, and that blood was the main source of their diet. While synthetic blood had been crafted in Sheol to deliver to demons who required it to survive, he couldn't get it while being topside, so he had to resort to using the old-fashioned method, which was hypnotizing humans into letting him take a pint from their vein.

Traditional vampire style.

"Thorne and his people are getting some drinks and snacks before joining us," he continued.

She nodded. "I went to knock on Rhys' door, but he didn't answer. I think he might be in the shower."

"I spoke to him on my way up here. He was heading out to join the Levis and Dagons for dinner at Hakkasan."

Remi's shoulders sagged at that. He hadn't told her. He hadn't even left a note or a text. That only further made her believe he was avoiding her. "I see," she murmured.

Quin watched her for several moments. Slowly, he lifted a shaking finger to her chin and raised it, something that had to be rubbing raw against his germaphobia. "What's wrong?" he asked, staring into her eyes. "You are…sad."

Remi stiffened, slamming her mental walls into place so fast that Quin's eyes widened in surprise. She forced a smile that she knew didn't reach her eyes. "I'm fine," she lied. She waved to the TV hanging on the wall. "Want to watch something while we wait on the others, or do you want to get a head start and jump in the pool?"

He didn't move, simply held her chin in place and watched her. "Remi," he murmured, stroking her skin with his thumb in an oddly intimate way, "you have witnessed the most embarrassing bits of my fear, and instead of laughing me in the face, you've helped me ease out of it little by little. Don't get me wrong, I still have quite a way to go, but thanks to your kindness and patience, I've made more progress in the last four days than I've made in years. You can trust me with anything, the way I've learned to trust you. If you have no one to relieve your burdens onto, at least know you can rely on me." Then, he grinned, holding his arms out wide. "All these muscles aren't just for show, you know. These shoulders double as comfort pillows."

Remi found herself smiling at his speech. With her djinni senses, she could see his heart was pure. It wasn't filled with greed or a desperate desire for anything more than to help people in pain. He really was a big softie, and that knowledge melted her heart. Without thinking, she leaned forward and wrapped her arms around him, snuggling her face into the hard planes of his chest while she allowed her walls to fall.

Quin hesitated, likely uncomfortable with the sudden contact, despite his offer to let her lean on him. After a moment, he patted her on the back with awkward movements. He side-walked them to the couches. Remi clung to him until he lowered himself onto one, pulling her down with him. She sat next to him, tucking her legs under her body and leaning into him while he stroked the top of her head.

It was…nice, not sexual or intimate or anything of the sort that one would think, just one friend comforting another. Had it been Rhys, she would have been turned on, eager to climb into his lap and ride him throughout the night. Hell, had it been two weeks ago she would have thought about doing the very same to Quin. He was gorgeous, sweet, funny and caring—but he wasn't Rhys. Oddly, he was the only man she wanted. It was a dangerous notion, but she couldn't find it in herself to care at the moment.

She heaved a deep sigh. She hadn't felt such a comfort in years—since she and her sister had been young teens, in fact. "I think Rhys is angry with me."

"What makes you think that?" Quin asked.

She snorted. "Have you seen the way he's been treating me? He hasn't even looked at me since Monday, and whenever he speaks to me, he's…cold, like I did something to piss him off."

"Hmm. What do you think it is that you've done?"

Remi hesitated, knowing Quin and Thorne shared the same hatred for the Belials as Rhys did. Their reactions would mirror Rhys' if they found out, but she found the words spilling from her lips. "Well…I may have gone to eat breakfast with Graham Belial that first morning."

Quin made a shocked noise in his throat, his stroking hand going still. "You *what*?"

"It was just breakfast," she said hastily. "Rhys was still asleep, and I wanted something to eat, but I got lost. Graham came up to me and offered to help, then invited me to breakfast. Don't get me wrong... I was going to turn him down, but I saw he was desperate for something and wanted to figure out what it was. When he introduced himself to me, I realized he might have been trying to plot something against EUC, so I decided to investigate for myself to see if I could find out what it was."

Quin released the breath he was holding, continuing to stroke her hair, though the moves were now stiff and jerky. "Good gods, woman. Didn't we tell you not to allow a Belial to get you alone? There's no telling what he could've done to you."

She snorted. "I may not have the powerful Lucifer blood on my side, but believe me when I say I'm not totally defenseless, Quinton."

He grunted. "It's Quin. And just because we're topside doesn't mean his powers can't work on you. He's still far more powerful than members not from the original families."

"Yeah, but he wasn't born topside, now, was he?"

Her sarcastic words caused him to stiffen again, and Remi belatedly realized what she'd said. She bit her lip and cursed herself for the revelation, but it was too late. The guilt flashing through her gave it away. Dammit, she should have kept her freaking defenses up.

Quin placed his hands on her shoulders and turned her so he could stare into her eyes. "You... You're from this realm?"

Remi tried to think of a lie to cover her ass, but she couldn't tell and untruth, not to Quin. His gaze held her captive, and deep within them he already knew the truth. There would be no persuading him into believing a lie. She sighed again, lowering her lashes. "Please don't tell anyone," she whispered, "especially Rhys."

Quin watched her for several minutes, his gaze searching for…something. Calculating. "Why would you hide something like this?" he demanded. "How the hell are you even allowed to live in Sheol?"

Remi ran a jittery hand through her hair, her eyes darting to the side. Crap on a freaking stick, this was what she'd been dreading for five years.

"I was disowned by my family years ago. My parents and I never got along, but I'd spent years studying and training hard to take over the family business, and when I was ready to do so, I learned it had all been for nothing. My parents refused to allow me or my sister to run the company. They wanted us to marry some rich snobs to increase their connections and allow our husbands to run everything, while we just sat back and looked pretty. I didn't want to live that kind of life, and when I fought against them, I was disowned for being 'too independent' and a disappointment to them. I didn't have anywhere else to go, but I'd heard a lot of talk about life in Sheol growing up. I wanted to embrace my demon side and live my own life, so…five years ago I traveled to Sheol."

He narrowed his eyes, questions swirling in the toffee depths. "What do you mean, 'embrace your demon side'? Are you a halfie? Furthermore, no one can travel to Sheol on a whim, and human money certainly doesn't work on the gatekeepers."

Remi remained silent, still tugging her hands through her hair. Dread was a twisted ball of dark energy in her gut, making her want to throw up. It was just as rare for demons born topside to pay even a short visit to Sheol, let alone take up permanent residence. The very, very few who did were elite members in Sheolic society with centuries' worth of accumulated wealth. Everyone knew that, which was the other reason why she was reluctant to tell anyone her secret.

"Remi," Quin said sternly. Then, he took her chin in his hand again. "You have my word this stays between us. On my honor as a Lucifer, I will not speak of this to another soul, not even my brothers. You can trust me."

Remi was shaking with fear all the way down to her bones, her reluctance to speak of her heritage to anyone twisting that ball of dread into a tighter knot. Not even Silas and Gracie knew the truth about her, and they'd been her closest friends for three years. She shifted on the couch, clasping her shaking hands in her lap. "I granted them a wish."

The very air in the room became so thick that it was suffocating.

"You're a djinni," Quin whispered, his voice so low that it was hard to tell if it was in surprise, awe or fear. *Probably a mix of all three.* Djinnis were pretty rare. Their wish-granting powers made them highly sought after by everyone, thus causing the need for them to keep their identities a secret.

Remi clutched her hands until her knuckles turned white. Since she was being truthful, she might as well go the rest of the way. She hoped Quin would keep his promise. "Half djinni, half shaman."

She knew the exact moment he pieced the puzzle together. His body jerked as if she'd slapped him. For the first time since she had been a little girl, Remi felt true terror seize her heart as she glanced up to see Quin's wide, horrified eyes. "You're Elizaroth's daughter, the djinni who left Sheol and married a human shaman half a century ago."

She gave a stiff nod. His mouth parted, working several times before more words were able to form. "Gods below... She was Hades' last-born child. You're the daughter of a demigod."

She lowered her chin, closing her eyes in dismay as the deepest, most safely guarded secret she'd hidden for decades came to light at last. "That would make me Hades' granddaughter by blood."

"Hell's fucking bells," Quin breathed.

Chapter Twelve

Rhys wasn't surprised to find the inside of the Sorrento Penthouse empty. Beyond the glass separating the patio from the living room, the gathering of his brothers and their officers had moved outside. Though he couldn't see them, he heard their splashing and loud chatter, followed by Thorne's boisterous laughter. Instead of joining the fun, Rhys went to his bedroom, tugging at his necktie to loosen it.

Exhaustion weighed his shoulders down as he kicked the door shut behind him and fell face-first onto the king-sized bed. He kicked his shoes off, not caring about scuffing the expensive leather. He wanted nothing more than to sleep for the next two hundred years, to push his duties off on someone else and let them deal with his bullshit.

He'd made the decision to stay away from Remi, a feat that was proving to be far more difficult than he cared to admit. Every time he heard her voice from a distance or got a whiff of her lingering sweet scent in the main room, his chest would clench with pain — a deep-rooted pain that resulted in the desire to seek her out, pull her into his arms and make love to her all night. Make *love*! He never, *ever* made love to anyone. Sex had always been a physical act to him, a means to find release before continuing on with his life.

Yet Remi wasn't just anyone. She was the one woman who'd managed to find a crack in the stone box around his heart and wriggle her way inside. She was witty and kind, patient and tender, smart and bold. She was perfect.

Though she drove him mad with desire, he had to acknowledge that he felt more at peace by her side than anywhere else. Her very presence drove away the darkness, the eternal stress that had been plaguing him for the last twenty years. It was like he could breathe around her, as if the depressing weight of his responsibilities became lighter.

And he no longer felt alone.

'Unlike you, I know full well when I meet a one-of-a-kind woman. And if you have no desire to take her, then I will. That's on my oath.'

Graham's solemn words echoed in Rhys' mind, taunting him. Rhys had been groomed from birth with the knowledge that he alone would have to take his father's role, and he had until his hundredth birthday to find a mate and do so. He'd been trained to only accept a woman whose birthing was of the highest standards, someone who had a surname that was widely known and respected throughout Sheol.

And while Rhys had met plenty of women who fit the bill, as well as having several lined up, thanks to his father's interference, he'd put it all off, wanting to wait until the very last day before his birthday to make it official. At that point, he would have blindfolded himself and chosen one of the women at random, because the outcome would be the same, regardless. They'd be two strangers forced into marriage for political gain, forever bound to one another in a loveless mating until one or the other of them died.

Rhys had accepted that fate long ago. He'd had no say in the matter, so he'd accepted the role as nothing more than another one of his responsibilities. However, things were different now. *He* was different. He didn't want that kind of life. He didn't want anything to do with any other woman. All he wanted was Remi. Even with her suspicious past, none of that mattered. He only wanted the beautiful redhead who'd captured his heart the moment he'd first laid eyes on her barking out orders to her coworkers.

Gods help me.

A knock sounded on his door, but the intruder didn't bother waiting for an answer. Whichever brother it was—Thorne, going by his scent—strolled in. "Get your sorry ass up and join the fun."

Something clomped against the back of Rhys' head, making him shout in pain. "What the fuck was that?" he growled, pushing himself up to rub his head. He glanced around the bed, gritting his teeth when he saw an empty glass beer bottle. He picked it up, glaring at Thorne. "You asshole."

Thorne looked far too comfortable for his own good, wearing only black swimming trunks. And he was dripping wet, right onto Rhys' floor. "What the hell, man? Get a towel and clean that shit up."

Thorne shook himself like a fucking dog, sending droplets of water everywhere. Then he grinned. "Nah,

I'm good. But you need to stop being an antisocial jagoff and come hang with us."

Rhys turned his back on Thorne, shrugging out of his suit jacket. "I have far too much work needing to be done than to waste time partying with the riffraff."

"Riffraff?" Thorne echoed, offended. "The hell? You need a good swim. Maybe it'll lube you up enough to finally get that stick out of your ass."

Rhys flipped him the bird. "Piss off," he grouched, stomping to the bathroom.

Of course, Thorne followed him. He was like a goddamned leech. It'd take a blowtorch to his skin to get him to go away. "It's because of Remi, isn't it? You're avoiding her."

Rhys stiffened over the threshold, his reaction giving him away. "I said piss off. It's none of your concern."

Thorne let out a loud bark of laughter, though there was no humor in the sound. "It becomes my concern when I see her sitting around moping over you when she's been a blast to have around these past few days."

He looked over his shoulder with surprise. "She's been moping over me?"

His brother scoffed in disbelief. "She's clearly into your ass, for gods only know why, and you've been avoiding her these last two days. Of course she's moping. Hell, I walked in on Quin comforting her because of you—"

"He *what*?" Rhys growled, whirling around completely. While logic told him that Quin was too much of a germaphobe to try to comfort someone with physical contact, it was the green part of him that conjured up different images of his brother holding

Remi, kissing her, touching her, stroking her in ways that would make her melt against him.

Thorne grunted in annoyance. "See? That just proves my point that you've fallen for her. You're jealous over your own brother, when if you would take the time to study the situation, you'd see Quin only sees Remi as a friend — and she him."

Rhys frowned, knitting his brows together. "He was lusting after her that first night at Stripsteak. I saw it."

"Did you see it? Or were you too drunk and lost in your own emotions to see the truth?" Thorne crossed his arms. "Quin's only interest in Remi is befriending her, just as it's the same with the rest of us. She's beautiful, sure, and any man in his right mind would be hell-bent on getting her attention, but anyone can look at either one of you and tell they don't stand a chance. Even I know not to cross that line. Every time you two look at each other, your eyes light up and you both get this sappy-ass look on your faces. Yet both of you are too damn stubborn to admit it — her because she doesn't want to get her heart broken and you because you have this bullshit mentality that you need some high-class broad on your arm to be considered a good ruler. You're both pissing me off. I'm trying to get drunk off my ass these next couple of nights and make the most of this damn convention, but you two are being absolute fucking buzzkills. Now stop feeling sorry for yourself, throw on some goddamn swimming trunks and get your ass out on the patio to fucking talk to her."

He turned away and stomped toward the door, pausing to glare over his shoulder with blazing eyes. "And if you aren't out there in the next ten minutes, so help me I will drag you out by your damned horns and toss you over the balcony." Threat delivered, he slammed the door shut and stormed away.

Rhys just stared after him with wide eyes. That was a first. Of the three of them, Thorne was always the one smiling and laughing, finding humor in everything when no one else did. He was one of those laid-back douchebags that everyone enjoyed hanging around with then wanted to punch in the face after a while, and he was even more reluctant to develop lingering feelings for women than Rhys was. And yet he'd just told Rhys off, revealing inner feelings Rhys had never known he had.

Furthermore, his brother's words stuck with him, because he was right. Well, he didn't know how true it was about Remi's feelings, but the rest of it was on point. Rhys *did* feel strongly about Remi. He couldn't lie about it anymore, not even to himself. He cared about her. Hell, more than that. He was in love with her.

Not that he had any prior experience to know what love felt like, but the gaping hole in his chest that could only be filled by Remi's touch and presence made him think it was love.

Did she really feel the same way about him? Despite their agreement weeks ago, was it possible that she'd developed the same feelings for him as he had for her? He wanted to know. No, he *needed* to know. He needed to know where she stood, and whether or not there was a possibility of a future for them.

Policies be damned. He didn't care about her ranking—or where she came from, or hell, if she only had two torqs to her name. Not anymore. He had enough wealth to provide them with a lifetime of comfort, and if his father had anything to say about it, he'd tell him to stick it where the sun doesn't shine. He'd even step down as ruler and allow one of his brothers or a distant cousin to take over. He only wanted Remi, and damn it all, he was going to show her just how perfect they were together.

But he couldn't just plain say it. He had to play his cards right and ease her into it. He'd have to coax her into opening up to him and allowing him inside so he could share his feelings with her. He needed her full trust so she would know he meant every word.

Nodding to himself, he disrobed and dug through the dresser that he'd packed his clothes into, pulling out his swimwear. He slid them on and grabbed a thick towel from the attached bathroom before making his way onto the terrace.

He glanced around the corner and saw Thorne, Quin and Desmond relaxing in the jacuzzi. In the pool, Bobby had Carmen on his shoulders, facing off against Colin, who was holding Maya on his. The women had their hands clasped, each trying to dismount the other. What was the game called again? Chicken something? Chicken match?

Rhys glanced around, frowning when he didn't see Remi.

"Sorry about that, guys. My friends called me with an update about my dog. I had to take it."

Rhys turned to spot Remi exiting the living room to step onto the terrace. He gulped, his entire body growing hard at the sight of her in a sexy bathing suit that revealed far more than it covered. It clung to her hourglass figure, the black color a stark contrast against her fair skin and flaming red hair. And speaking of her hair, she'd left it loose to flow around her in soft curls, the gentle breeze of the spring air blowing the silky strands to the side.

Gods below, she is so beautiful. The sight of her with the soft glow of the pool light and the light shining from the living room shrouded her in an almost celestial way. It was a perfect candid moment. An image flashed in his mind, a longing to throw her over his shoulder, carry her to his room and ravish her on his bed — and in the shower, and on the couch, the dining room table, the Jacuzzi. Hell, even on the stairs. The list was endless.

Remi glanced up, blinking in surprise to see him standing there. "Oh, hi," she murmured.

"Hi," he responded lamely. He cleared his throat. "Do you want to talk?"

She stiffened, fear flashing in her eyes. "A-about what?" Her eyes darted to the side then back at him.

He frowned, wondering if his standoffish attitude toward her had put her on edge. It was hard to say since he still couldn't read her. The only bit of feelings he could get from her was what showed in her expressive eyes that were a murky green color. "I wanted to apologize for the way I've acted these last couple of days. I realize it must have been...strange."

"Oh," she breathed, an odd look of relief crossing her features. She relaxed, giving him an easy smile that didn't quite reach her eyes. "Apology accepted." Then she sauntered down the steps and headed for the pool chairs on the far side of the terrace.

Rhys frowned after her, trying to keep his eyes from dropping to her beautiful ass. He failed, of course. But his worry over her nonchalant attitude trumped his physical needs. He wondered if she truly had forgiven him. Somehow, he didn't think so. He missed the witty banter and dry remarks she usually gave him.

He looked at Thorne in question. His brother only glared and jerked his chin in Remi's direction, silently telling him to get a move on. Squaring his shoulders, Rhys followed her to the edge of the pool, taking a seat in the chair next to her. They were far enough away from the others to grant them privacy to speak to one another.

She raised an eyebrow at him in question. "Aren't you going to get in the water?"

"Aren't you?" he countered.

"Eventually. I'm waiting on this fight to end so I can take the next round."

Rhys eyed Colin and Bobby, jealousy once again rearing its head. Having Remi's legs straddling another man's neck while her core pressed against his head? *Fuck no.* He gave a tight smile. "Why wait? We can join the fun. It can be a three-way match."

She glanced at him in suspicion. "*You* want to join in?" She waved her hands in front of his face, then placed her palm on his forehead. "Are you fevered? Did you drink too much at dinner?"

Rhys scowled, grasping her wrist to tug it away. "No need to act so surprised. I'm not so uptight that I don't know when to let my horns down."

"Yes, you are," Remi said with absolute certainty. She peered down at where he held her, stroking his thumb over her inner wrist. She still watched him with skepticism, though her eyes were turning brown with arousal. "Are you okay?"

No, I'm not.

He was nervous that she was going to reject him and his feelings. He was hot and bothered at the sight of her in her sexy bathing suit. He was annoyed that they weren't alone so he could turn his charm to the highest degree and seduce her into his bed. "I'm perfectly fine," he whispered, dropping his gaze to her full lips when her tongue darted out to wet them. He almost groaned aloud.

"You have that look," she whispered.

"What look?"

"The one where it looks like you want to take a bite out of me."

"Hmm. What if I do?"

Her breath hitched a little. "Then I'd say —"

"Hey, if you two are going to fuck, take it inside," Carmen shouted.

Remi's cheeks turned a bright shade of red, and Rhys was sure his weren't looking much different as they pulled away from each other, like two embarrassed teenagers caught doing something they shouldn't have been.

He cleared his throat, nodding at the pool. "What do you say? Want to partner up for this chicken scratch?"

She shook her head and stood with a small smile. "It's chicken *fight*. And yes. Let's kick their asses."

Chapter Thirteen

It was after midnight when everyone returned to their individual rooms. Well, almost everyone. Quin and Thorne had gone upstairs and passed out in the spare bedrooms, and Maya had been far too drunk to move much farther than the couch, so she'd crashed in the living room.

Remi'd had only one Corona, so she wasn't even slightly buzzed. Still, she'd enjoyed herself, more so after Rhys had joined them and participated in their silly games. Like her, he'd drunk very little, and they'd spent a good bit of the time talking about anything and everything for hours, up until they realized they were the only ones left awake.

At that point, Remi had realized how late it was and had bidden him goodnight. Though he'd looked disappointed, he hadn't tried to change her mind, and so allowed her to go to her room to shower and change into a simple silk slip. She threw on a fresh terrycloth robe over it, tightening the belt at her waist before making her way downstairs. Despite how late it was, she wasn't tired at all. Quite the opposite, in fact. Her body was buzzing with energy, her nerve endings racing.

She had been nervous ever since telling Quin the truth about her heritage. Though she trusted him not to tell anyone her secrets, she'd still been paranoid all night that someone else was going to find out. Suddenly everyone would want her to grant them a wish or for her to get them in Hades' good graces – not that she'd ever met the god – or anything along those selfish lines.

She wouldn't be Remington Sawyer anymore, the data entry clerk who'd spent three years working on the lower level of EUC. No, she'd only be known as Hades' granddaughter or the daughter of Elizaroth. The reputation and easy relationships with her coworkers she'd worked so hard to build would come crumbling down. No one would ever again think of her as just Remi.

Not for the first time, she regretted not being normal and born from a regular low-class demon couple. No, it had to be a freaking runaway deity and a shaman, two creatures who should have never crossed paths, yet had done so and wound up married, thus producing offspring that could never truly belong to any world. Despite being a half-blood, Remi had inherited her mother's djinni powers, making her more demon than human. On the other hand, her sister Jericho had inherited their father's powers, making her more human than demon, which in turn had made her life topside far easier for her. Remi, however, had always felt the need to be in Sheol, the heart-wrenching desire to make a life in her mother's homeland one that had been within her since she was a child, since the first day she'd gotten mad at a local human boy and he'd seen her eyes turn red.

Heaving a deep sigh, she made it to the ground floor and padded into the kitchen, tiptoeing to try not to wake up Maya. Well, the panther was pretty much dead to the world, lying face-down and snoring like a bear, so Remi doubted the woman would wake, even if a band of centaurs came galloping through. The thought made her snort with laughter as she opened the refrigerator door.

It had been stocked with food and drinks earlier in the week, so Remi spent several moments peering inside, then bent over to study the bottom shelves as she tried to figure out what to eat.

She didn't hear anyone approach her, not until someone let out a soft whistle of appreciation. Glancing over her shoulder, she spotted Rhys standing at the kitchen's entrance, leaning against the wall with a wide grin. He was shirtless, dressed only in a pair of black boxer briefs. Remi's mouth went dry, and suddenly she didn't care about food anymore. She had an appetite for something else.

Meeting his heated gaze, she smiled and wiggled her ass, much like she'd done when they'd first had sex. "Like what you see, bossman?" she teased.

"Immensely," he murmured, pushing away from the wall. He walked up to her and stood until his crotch pressed against her. Remi's panties grew damp as heat shot straight to her core. He smoothed his hands over her back, gently grinding into her. The robe should have prevented her from feeling much, but it didn't. She felt everything almost as easily as if she were naked. "What are you still doing up?"

"Looking for a snack," she murmured…or moaned. It was a cross between the two. "You?"

"Same," he husked, gripping her waist. He made her straighten so he could close the fridge door, then he pinned her against it with his body. "I've just found what I have a taste for."

Remi palmed the hard muscles of his chest, running her fingers across the smooth stretch of skin. Feeling brave, she leaned forward and flicked her tongue over one of his nipples, drawing a sharp gasp. She flashed a wicked grin. "As have I," she murmured, doing the same to the other. She placed a gentle kiss to the space between his pecs while sliding her hands downward.

His toned stomach tightened when her light touch trailed to the waistband of his briefs. She followed the same path with her lips until she was on her knees before him. He gasped, grasping her upper arms. "Remi," he breathed, looking down at her with dark eyes.

"Let me," she murmured. Still holding his gaze, she placed a kiss to the erection popping a tent before her. "I want to."

He swallowed audibly, releasing her. Smiling, Remi kissed him again, caressing his muscular thighs, calves, ankles, then back up to the hem of his shorts. With a small tug, she jerked them down, freeing the massive cock that already had a bead of moisture at its tip.

With one hand, she grabbed him by the base of his shaft, holding him still as she tasted him. He jerked, a strangled noise rumbling inside his chest as she circled her tongue around the mushroom-like head. Then she closed her lips over him, slowly drawing them down until they met her fist at his base.

Rhys let out a long sigh, throwing his head back as she worked her mouth and hand over him in a synchronized rhythm. His desire fueled her own, the sight of his expression filled with pleasure causing dampness to pool between her legs. When she flattened her tongue against him and relaxed her throat to take as much as she could, he fisted in her hair and a small choked sound escaped his mouth. "Oh hell, baby," he growled in soft tones, trying not to be overheard.

While she focused on keeping her gag reflexes from making her tap out, she slid her tongue along the underside of his shaft as he pumped into her mouth with short strokes. He tensed as he prepared to come, his breathing coming out in ragged pants. When she reached up to roll his sac between her fingers, he froze, shooting jets of his hot seed into her mouth.

And Remi continued to suck. He tightened his grasp on her hair, holding her head in place until she'd swallowed every last drop. With a satisfied smile, she sat back on her heels, prepared to say something witty.

She was cut out with a squeak of surprise when he jerked her to her feet, once more pinning her to the fridge. He buried his face in her neck, kissing and sucking her skin with a fevered passion. He roamed his hands everywhere, stroking her breasts, squeezing her ass, caressing her hair. When he gripped the back of one of her legs and pulled it around his waist, she gasped at the feeling of his still-erect cock pressing against her.

"I need to be inside you," he growled in her ear, nipping her lobe before drawing it into his mouth. "I need to feel your heat soaking my dick while I make you scream my name."

His words damn near turned her into a puddle of her own juices. "Yes," she breathed, wrapping her arms around his neck.

He growled in approval and scooped her into his arms. Proving he was anything but human, all it took was a single blink and they were in his room. He kicked the door shut and locked it, then tossed her into the middle of the king-size bed. Before she could move, he followed her, covering her body with his much larger one. He untied the belt of her robe and drew it open, then fisted her slip with both hands. "On a scale of one to ten, how much do you like this thing?"

"About a six, but—"

Rhys ripped her silky gown in half, then her panties. "Hey!" she protested.

"I'll buy you another one," he murmured, kissing her inner thigh. "I'll buy you a hundred of them. I promise. But right now, I can't wait. I need to taste you."

He forced her legs apart and dragged his tongue down her inner thigh, teasing the back of her knee, down the smooth skin of her leg—thank the gods she'd waxed before the trip—and to her feet. Remi expected the teasing to end there, but it didn't. Holding her gaze, he trailed his tongue over the top of her foot until he drew her toes into his mouth. She gasped at the erotic sensation, never before having had a man do that to her. He switched his attention to her other foot, giving it the same attention in reverse.

Remi thought he would he would finally put his tongue where she needed him the most, but no. He gripped her waist and flipped her over, pulling her hips up as if he was going to take her from behind. She jumped with surprise when he spread her legs farther and touched her slit with the tip of his tongue. She cried out as he pleasured her in a way that was unfamiliar to her, yet it felt so damn amazing.

He kneaded her thighs and ass with his hands while he continued to suck and lick her essence. Remi pressed her face into the pillow to muffle her cries, but she jerked with a squeak when he slapped his hand across her backside. It wasn't hard enough for it to hurt, but it was the right amount of pleasure-pain that almost sent her toppling over the edge into bliss. "Why?" she moaned, unable to form much more than that.

He rubbed over the spot he'd rapped, pulling away from her dripping sex, much to her frustration. "Don't block your moans," he commanded. "I want to hear every noise you make."

"But the others—"

"I don't care if you wake up everyone in this hotel," he interrupted. He leaned forward to blow on her, the chill sending a delicious shiver up her spine. "I told you I want you screaming my name." With that, he once again placed his mouth on her, the warm cavern a stark contrast against the chill he'd caused. She released a drawn-out moan, arching forward to raise her ass even higher.

Rhys was relentless as he tortured her in the best way, and when she pressed her face into the pillows, he popped her again, this time making her cry out as an orgasm tore through her. Before she was done, he flipped her onto her back and buried himself inside her in one smooth motion. She gasped at the penetration, his size stretching her, even though he'd made sure she was sopping wet.

"Fuck," he breathed, rocking his hips into her. He leaned forward with his forearms on either side of her head, caging her in. His eyes were black, completely swallowed by the pupils as he was consumed with lust. Remi was sure hers looked pretty similar, the brown surely spreading over the green as pleasure swamped her. Had they not been wearing the glamour necklaces, however, they both would have had gleaming red eyes.

With his nose an inch from hers, their breaths mingling with each exhale, Rhys rocked into her with slow, teasing movements. They'd both had fast orgasms, and it seemed he wanted to drag out the next one. Her body was still heated, eager for another dive over the cliff of pure ecstasy. But he just moved with agonizing slowness, his half-mast eyes never once looking away from hers.

"You're so beautiful," he whispered in awe.

Remi stroked her hands over his shoulders, down his arms, then back up. His words threatened to break the resolve she'd always kept around her heart with past lovers. "You are too," she murmured.

Something shifted deep within his eyes, as if her words touched him — which was ridiculous, wasn't it? They'd agreed on nothing more than a physical relationship. Just casual encounters.

Except nothing about his actions felt casual — not the way he touched her, not the way he spoke to her and certainly not the way he rolled his hips into her, whispering soft compliments that made her heart melt, which was terrifying because nothing about her should be melting for this man except for her libido.

And yet everything was. Something had changed, something that frightened her far more than having all of Elysium finding out who she was. At that moment, Rhys had total power over her body, mind and soul. Somewhere in the last few weeks, he'd taken something from her, something that left her vulnerable and open to the possibility of encountering the worst pain she'd ever feel — heartbreak.

He leaned forward and tentatively pressed his lips to hers as if he wasn't accustomed to kissing. He learned fast, however. He kissed her once, twice, three times. "Sh-h, love," he murmured against her mouth. "Don't think. Just feel. Feel this," he rolled into her with more force, drawing a gasp from her. "Feel me. Feel *us*." He kissed her again. "I've never felt anything like this."

Somehow Remi got the sense he wasn't talking about their actual lovemaking. He meant something deeper, something far more dangerous that went beyond physical acts. "What does it feel like?" she asked, her voice letting out the slightest of trembles.

"New. Terrifying." He paused his hips, still buried deep within her. His eyes were wondrous. "But I don't want it to go away."

Remi gulped, her heart clenching because, gods forbid, she was falling for him. Hell, she already had. "Neither do I," she whispered, so softly that if he hadn't read her lips, he would have never heard it.

It was his turn to swallow. He kissed her again, deepening it while he stroked into her much faster than before. He shot his tongue past her lips, tangling with hers. She rested her hands on his shoulders as he fucked her, pushing deeper with each drive forward. He slid one arm under her leg, drawing her knee to her chest as he picked up speed.

Remi moaned as his blows grew faster, sometimes withdrawing completely before plunging back in, sometimes giving her short thrusts that drove her mad. He released her leg and slid his arm under her back, holding her as close as possible while she wrapped her legs around his waist, digging her nails into his back and shoulders.

They were panting, both of them so close to another climax. Rhys kissed her neck. "Come for me, love," he commanded in her ear. "Let me take you to a place where no man ever has."

She curled one hand around the nape of his neck as he pounded into her. "Yes, Rhys. Don't... Please... don't... Ah!" Rhys slammed his lips against hers, swallowing her cry as the most explosive orgasm of her life rippled through her, a never-ending wave of ecstasy that sent her soaring through the night sky.

"Oh, damn," Rhys growled. "You're so fucking beautiful." He tensed, shoving his shaft as deep into her as he could as his own climax claimed him. He gave a strangled shout, cutting it off by biting into the side of her neck, the same as he'd done the first time they'd had sex. Unlike that time, however, Remi felt pain, as if he'd bitten through skin.

Still, she was floating too high to care. She didn't mind a little pain with sex. All she knew was the sweet bliss of being held in Rhys' arms. He collapsed on top of her, rolling onto his side and pulling her close. "Stay with me," he whispered against her forehead, his breath hot against her skin. He placed a chaste kiss there and exhaled a long, slow breath.

Remi relaxed, curling her arms around him as he tightened his around her, as if afraid she'd disappear the moment he let go. "You mean for tonight?" she asked, a yawn forming on the last word.

He stroked her hair, his breathing slowing until he fell asleep. Remi was dozing off as well, but just before slumber claimed her, she thought she heard his faint whisper.

"Forever."

Chapter Fourteen

For the first time in decades, Rhys awoke feeling sated, rested and...happy.

He cracked his eyes open, a smile curling the corner of his lips when he saw Remi was still in bed with him, fast asleep. She was lying on her back, though the hand closest to him was curled around his own, their fingers loosely intertwined.

With morning sunlight spilling in from the open drapes, the bright rays shone an almost ethereal light on her porcelain skin. Her lashes lay still over her high cheekbones dotted with a light dusting of pale freckles, her nose a fine noble swoop, her full lips red and swollen from his kisses the previous night. Her hair was left loose to flow over the pillows around her, giving her the appearance of some kind of regal fire goddess.

Gods above and below, she is exquisite. Beautiful. And all his.

He trailed his gaze to the crook where her shoulder and neck met. A round bite mark rested there, a bruise from his getting carried away. He reached a shaking finger to touch it, guilt and worry and pride flooding through him. Pride, because at long last he'd claimed the perfect woman as his mate.

However, guilt and worry warred within him, taking away what should have been a joyous occasion. Though he and Remi had connected in a way only two hearts could, he hadn't received her permission to claim her, to mark his territory to keep all other males away. They hadn't declared eternal love and devotion to one another, yet he was tied to her until the next full moon. If she didn't agree to be his mate by then, his seal on her would be broken, and the potential mating would come to a painful end for him. He wouldn't die, but he might feel like it. Until she either accepted or denied him, there would never be another for him.

Although, if he were being honest with himself, it was already too late for that, with or without the marking.

What was worse, he wasn't sure how she would react to the news, but he was positive she wouldn't take it well. She'd kept her feelings on a tight leash, keeping herself as guarded as he had. Even if he dropped to his knees and begged her to give him a chance, to accept all the love and protection he was willing to give her, there was also the matter that she would be agreeing to rule Elysium with him, something that she wasn't trained to do as he was.

He placed a kiss to her fingers holding his, then gently slid out of bed so as to not disturb her. She was going to see the mark once she woke up. That was inevitable. All he could hope for was to keep her calm and explain what was occurring and try to persuade her into seeing that they were perfect together. It went beyond sex. The chemistry between them, the way they made each other smile and laugh, the easy connection they'd formed right from the start? The gods themselves couldn't have made a better match.

Inhaling a shaky breath, he prayed to Hades to grant him the strength and courage he needed to get through this. Because if Remi didn't agree to be his mate, then his world was going to return to its normal, bleak state. Only this time he'd have to go on with a broken heart that would never heal.

Before he made it to the connecting bathroom, he paused when his phone buzzed on the nightstand. He picked it up, seeing he had thirty missed calls. *Thirty!* Half of them from Kelle, several from his work associates down below and a handful from an unknown Sheolic number.

He called his assistant first, strolling toward the bathroom. Kelle answered on the first ring. "Rhys, please tell me you saw the emails I've sent you!"

He frowned at the breathless excitement in Kelle's tone, running the water in the large shower stall to a steamy temp. "No, I only just woke up. What is it?"

"Gods, I don't even know where to begin! Gunter and I have been trying to contact you all night. You have to go check your email."

He blinked in confusion. "Who the hell is Gunter?"

Kelle made a sound of frustration. "The PI you asked me to hire to get some info on Remington Sawyer."

"Ah. Has he found anything?" he asked, leaving the bedroom and to go to the living room where he'd left his laptop on the coffee table. He glanced around and saw the room was empty, meaning Maya had awoken at some point and returned to her room.

"Obviously!" Kelle exclaimed. "You really are daft this morning. Check out those emails and call me back. Gunter's waiting to collect his payment."

Rhys just grunted a response and disconnected the line as he opened his computer. It took several moments for the startup screen to pop up, and with one click he was pulling up his emails. He had several, most of them dealing with BS business he didn't feel like responding to at the moment. He clicked on the latest one from Kelle, which contained a link to an encrypted website.

For several moments, he frowned, confusion swamping him as the link brought him to the homepage of Sawconn Global, some kind of uppity oil and gas company. He squinted his eyes as he scrolled through, reading over the rather impressive statistics of what had started out as a small, ordinary couple living in Saudi Arabia becoming filthy rich after a stroke of luck showed that they owned a good bit of land above a massive oil field discovered some fifty years ago.

The company had been passed down to the couple's grandson Rueben Sawyer and his wife, Eliza. Rhys clicked on the 'About Us' tab and scrolled down to see an image of the current family — Rueben, Eliza and their adult daughter, Jericho. The image was creepy as hell, as even with a glance he could tell their wide smiles were fake. There was an austere, desolate look in their eyes, and the daughter looked like she'd rather be anywhere else except there.

He still didn't know what he was looking at. He called Kelle. "What is this?" he demanded.

"I thought the name would be a dead giveaway," she drawled. "Those are the Sawyers. As you can see, there is only one image of the family. If you type them into Google—er, the human version of Boogle—you'll only find that one image. All of their social media sites, news articles, everything on them has that one picture."

"And? Is that strange?" He didn't like taking pictures himself. He knew he couldn't be the only one.

"What's strange is that there are no other picture of them, not even the original founders of Sawconn Global fifty years ago."

He frowned, a headache forming behind his skull. Making his exasperation clear, he asked, "What has any of this to do with what Dietrich found?"

Kelle sighed as if *he* was the vexing one. "Those are Remi's parents and sister. She's the eldest by three years, but they removed her from the image years ago to make it seem as though she doesn't exist."

He sat back, his eyes widening. "What?" Rage fought against confusion. His anger was directed at how heartless Remi's family could be to cut her out of their lives. Literally. Nothing was making sense, and that was pissing him clean off. He glanced over his shoulder to make sure no one was spying, then lowered his voice to a hiss. "You mean to tell me she was born topside?"

"Oh, that's just the tip of the iceberg, Rhys. Check the other email we sent you."

Rhys did as he was told. It had an attachment, and he hovered the mouse over the paperclip to bring the image to life. What he saw was a side-by-side comparison of an old painting of a beautiful female djinni surrounded by lesser demons bowing at her feet and a close-up image of Eliza Sawyer. The djinni was a woman who was known far and wide across Sheol, though not many people had ever seen her in person. She was Hades' last daughter, a djinni demigod who had the power to grant wishes of the heart in exchange for a high price — usually requiring a sacrifice or two.

As the story went, some fifty years ago she had been summoned by a powerful shaman to the human world, and instead of returning to her home in Tartarus, the two had fallen in love and decided to elope, going against Hades' commands. Since they were in the human world, the 'free zone' between Sheol and Canaan that neither side had a true claim to, the dark god hadn't been able to do a damn thing about it.

Rhys studied the image of Elizaroth and Eliza. The resemblance was uncanny, to say the least. Though Eliza was blonde and bustier than the painting of the djinni with red hair, it was far too close to be a mere coincidence. Plus, the names were a dead fucking giveaway.

Then all the pieces slid into place. "Bloody hell," he breathed. If Remi was Eliza Sawyer's daughter, that meant she was Elizaroth's daughter, which in turn made her Hades' granddaughter — his *real* granddaughter.

Not only was Remi an heiress to a multi-million-dollar human company, she was also a direct descendant of one of the most powerful gods in existence.

Holy gods below. That also meant Remi outranked all four of the regal families, yet she'd spent the last three years working as an ordinary data entry clerk. The more he thought about it, the more everything about her began to make sense — her ability to handle her jobs with incredible ease, the simple way she was able to block his powers, the way all the demons who'd ventured topside for the convention were drained and easily inebriated, yet she was the only one full of energy, despite being the heaviest drinker.

"Kelle," he said sternly, remembering she was still on the phone. He shut his computer off and slammed the screen shut, then hid it under the couch. "*No one* is to find out about this, under any circumstance. Tell Dietrich I'll provide him with three passes for his silence. If word gets out about this… Hell, I don't even want to think about what kind of chaos would ensue. I want her reputation protected at all costs."

Kelle was silent for several moments, so long that Rhys feared she would disobey for the first time since he'd met her. Then, she chuckled with glee. "You're so in love with her. Oh, I never thought I'd see the day. Someone finally managed to crawl under your skin. Don't worry. I'm deleting all traces of this info as we speak. Good luck, Rhys."

"Thanks," he muttered, not even bothering to lie to Kelle about his feelings for Remi. According to Thorne, everyone already knew — or they could guess. He hung up the phone and stood, raking his hands through his hair.

It was just his luck. Remi was Hades' fucking granddaughter. He'd fallen in love with a woman who was part-deity. Not only that, but he'd marked her as his own before the great lord had ever gotten to meet her and give his approval.

What the fuck have I gotten myself into?

* * * *

Remi awoke to the smell of French toast, eggs, bacon and citrusy fruit. Peeling her eyes open, she sat up with a yawn to find she was still in Rhys' bed, which meant she hadn't dreamed of the wonderful, passionate sex they'd had. The thought made her smile, though wariness lingered in her heart. What if she was the only one who'd felt those emotions the previous night? What if it had only been a regular encounter for him? Hell, if that were the case, the man should have stuck with wild, impersonal sex instead of the slow, sensual lovemaking he'd given her.

She groaned, forcing back her fear as she took in the breakfast platter near the foot of the bed. Her stomach growled with anticipation.

"Good morning," Rhys greeted her, exiting the bathroom. He only wore dark dress pants and black socks, the top half of him left bare. "Did you sleep well?"

"Yes," she murmured. Her eyes were glued to the sculpted pecs, her mouth watering for something other than food.

Rhys' lips quirked into a half-smile, one that didn't quite reach his eyes. That wasn't a good sign. Her stomach knotted with fear, anxiety screaming that last night's emotional ride had been one-sided. She opened her djinni senses to see what was weighing on his heart, but all that was present was a strong desire to be near her. The thought should have comforted her, and in a way it did, but she got the feeling something was wrong.

He sat beside her on the bed and took her hand in his. "I ordered breakfast and drew you a bath so you can relax before the meeting."

Remi nodded, watching as he brought her hand to his lips and kissed each of her knuckles. "Are you okay?" she murmured, unable to shake the paranoid feeling that he was hiding something.

Her suspicions only grew when he hesitated. "I'm fine. There's just something I want to discuss with you in private, but it's best to wait until tonight."

Oh, gods.

It was time for The Talk, the dreaded conversation she'd always initiated with past lovers, but had never been on the receiving end. She squeezed his hand, although fear was a living entity in her chest. "I know what that means. If you're going to say something like, *'Hey, last night was fun, but we should end things'* and *'It's not you, it's me,'* then there's no need. I can take a hint." She patted him on the shoulder as if he were her old-time buddy and not a cherished lover.

He lifted a dark eyebrow, humor lighting his eyes. When he spoke, however, his tone was solemn. "I *do* want to talk about last night." He slid a finger under her chin and tilted her face toward his. Slowly, as if giving her time to pull away, he placed a lingering kiss to her lips. It was a soft brush, but Remi felt it all the way down to her curling toes. He pulled back, gazing deep into her eyes. "But I have no desire to end things with you, Remi. I…" He hesitated, and for a moment she held her breath as she thought he was going to say he loved her. Instead, he exhaled, giving her another brief kiss before standing. "We'll talk after the meeting. I promise. For now, enjoy your breakfast and bath, and I'll meet you in the conference room."

With that, he left the room and closed the door. Several moments later, she heard another door close — the entrance to the penthouse.

Disappointment rocked through her that he hadn't said the words she longed to hear. After peeking inside his heart, she knew he cared about her. He hadn't said it aloud, but he'd shown her with every touch. There was something that had been tying the two of them together, and after the previous night, she could no longer deny her feelings for him.

She was in love with Rhys Lucifer—completely, hopelessly, madly in love with a devil. Her boss. The soon-to-be ruler of Elysium.

But did he love her back? *Could* he love her? And if so, what would become of them? Spend some time dating to see where it went? If that were the case, how long could she keep her secret from him? How would he react when he found out? Would he only try to use her for his own personal gain before tossing her aside?

Hell, was he even now doing that? She'd hypothesized that he was trying to seduce her into agreeing to become his COO, but how far did she think he would go? Was this his plan all along? Make her fall hard for him before revealing his grand scheme?

So many questions circled through her brain, each one twisting the ball of trepidation tighter and tighter until breathing became a struggle.

Gods, she needed to calm down. Maybe she was overthinking everything. What happened to that everlasting cool-headedness she'd spent decades perfecting?

Give her a mountain of paperwork and a close-neck deadline to complete it all—no problem. Hand her a mile-long list of tasks to do with an inexperienced crew of workers to split the workload among—piece of cake. Throw the word 'love' in the air and tell her to either dodge or catch it—*bam*! Colossal meltdown on Aisle Remi.

With a deep groan, she scrubbed her eyes with the heels of her palms, then slid out of bed. She rolled the cart of food into the bathroom. The black marble around the jacuzzi-tub had a few lit tea candles around it, and the sweet smell of honeysuckle rose from the bubble bath. It was her favorite scent. She didn't know how the cunning devil knew — or if perhaps it was just a lucky guess on his end — but she didn't question it.

She didn't question anything as she stepped into the tub. There would be time for that later. She just wanted to relax and gather her bearings. The water warmed her as she sank into it. She leaned her head back and closed her eyes as she dissolved into utter peace.

Chapter Fifteen

The meeting had been by far the longest of the week, for which Remi had been thankful. The lengthy assembly had provided a nice distraction from stressing over her inner turmoil. It was the last day of the convention, since Friday would just be a closing dinner banquet.

All in all, the entire convention hadn't been as eventful as Rhys had exaggerated two weeks before. She'd had a lot to do, of course, what with providing support for Rhys and hastily throwing together a presentation that showed graphs of the incline in mortal death tolls over the past year. However, the time had seemed to fly. She'd met all forty-something attendees, had accepted business cards and invitations from several of them that would help her build personal connections between the four regions and even exchanged phone numbers with a few of them to set up luncheons and just 'hang out' when they visited the neighboring region.

She'd even won the favor of the Belials, having acted as a sort of mediator between them and the Lucifers. Of course, there was no patching up thousands of years' worth of contempt between the two families in just four days, but both sides had communicated without breaking out into a massive brawl, as had been the case at each of the past Séance Conventions. Of course, death threats and snippy insults had been thrown between the two families, but at least physical violence hadn't erupted. That was *something*.

Then again, Graham Belial had flirted with her more than a few times, which had made Rhys appear to nearly throttle the male, though tonight he'd been much more open about his feelings for her. The thought made Remi smile.

Now she was back in their shared penthouse suite. She'd left dinner ahead of him and several others from the other three regions to retire for the night. It was only a quarter past eight, but she wanted to rest her feet after standing in heels most of the day.

With a deep sigh, her former nervousness returned, though it was lighter now. Rhys had acted as if everything was normal, though he'd touched her as often as he could. A hand to her lower back as he guided her through doors, a gentle hand to her elbow, a brush of the back of his fingers against hers when they stood side-by-side. He'd even dabbed at her chin with a napkin at dinner when she'd dropped a small dot of pudding from her spoon.

That tender action had sent the entire table into an immediate silence, everyone staring between them. Rhys hadn't seemed to care as he continued eating his food, and Remi had tried doing the same, but it was hard to keep an appetite when everyone was watching her with critical eyes. She didn't need to be psychic to know what they were all thinking.

Shaking her head at the memory, she kicked off her heels and made her way over to the couch. Her new friends were dropping by, of course, so she wanted to kick her feet up and watch TV until then.

She wove her way around the sectionals to sit on the middle couch, but the sound of something cracking followed by a sharp pain under her foot made her yelp. She flopped down on the seat, then brought her foot up to massage her heel. Grunting with annoyance, she looked down to see what had assaulted her.

The corner of Rhys' computer peeked from under the couch. Annoyance forgotten, she slid it out, worrying she'd cracked the screen or broken it somehow. "Oh no. Please don't tell me I have to buy him another one," she muttered. She wouldn't be able to afford it. Everything Rhys owned was top-of-the-line, the absolute best of the best. His high-tech computer probably cost more than an entire month's apartment rent.

"Shit," she breathed, setting the apparatus on the glass coffee table in front of her. She flipped it open. Studying it, she released a happy, relieved breath of air when she saw the screen was perfectly intact. *Thank freaking gods*!

She reached for the top of the screen to close it and return it back under the couch — *why the hell was it under there anyway?* — but she froze as the screen came to life. Since it was his personal computer that no one would dare try to steal, Rhys hadn't bothered to put a password lock on it, so his last activity was still up. In any other circumstance, Remi would have closed it, not one for snooping in other people's privacy. However, the image on the screen sent a giant lump of coal to the bottom of her stomach.

The image was a side-by-side comparison of two women from two different eras. One was an old painting of a slim redhead, the other a clear, recent image of a curvy blonde. Though mortals would just assume the two women coincidentally looked similar, Remi knew better.

The two pictures were of the same woman — Elizaroth of Tartarus, also known as Eliza Sawyer in the modern day. Her mother.

With a shaking hand, Remi swiped her finger across the touchpad and clicked off, revealing Rhys' latest emails. Only two were opened, both from his assistant Kelle.

She clicked on the first, which was a forwarded email from someone named G. Dietrich. It was a link to her family's website. She didn't need to click on it. She recognized the domain, since she'd gone to it multiple times in the past five years.

However, the words in the email were what caused the breath in her lungs to go still.

Good day, Mr. Lucifer. I hope you find this information as satisfactory as I have. I'll be expecting my payment by next Friday. Thank you for your business.
Gunter Dietrich
Owner and Co-founder of Dietrich Investigative Services

Remi scanned through the text. It was like one of those revealing movie scenes, the ones where a character would read some kind of article and keywords would jump out at them. Hades. Elizaroth is

Eliza Sawyer. Granddaughter. Half-human, half-djinni. Remington Sawyer.

Rhys knew. God below, the devil knew who she was. He *knew*.

The memories from the previous night came roaring to life. He'd spent the last two days ignoring her existence, then, all of a sudden, he'd had a change of heart when he'd decided to join them by the poolside. She looked at the timestamp of when the emails had been sent. Wednesday at five p.m., hours before he'd joined them.

Then the special attention he'd given her the previous night... The passionate lovemaking, the tender confession that he'd never felt that way before, the whispered 'forever' as he asked her to stay with him... The loving gestures he'd shown her all day, making it seem as though he'd fallen in love with her after formerly declaring they would seek only a physical relationship...

Everything was far too much to be a coincidence. It didn't take a fucking genius to put two and two together. The timelines matched. Hell, hadn't she been suspicious that he had been acting strange earlier, that he was hiding something? This *had* to be it.

So, it had all been a lie. He'd found the truth about her heritage, about just how high her demon ranking was compared to his, and he'd taken full advantage of it. He'd lied and used her, just as she'd feared. He'd made her fall in love with him for his own interests.

That lying, conniving, shady asshole!

He was a fucking Lucifer, all right—a scheming, two-faced bastard who'd pulled the dirtiest of tricks.

Remi was absolutely livid. She fisted her hands in her lap to keep from shaking with rage, but it was a failed attempt.

And yet, she couldn't stop the tears spilling from her eyes. Her heart shredded itself, squeezing in her chest until she felt like she was going to pass out from lack of air.

It was just too freaking bad that she couldn't grant her own wishes. While djinni magic wouldn't work against other people's demise or change their feelings, it was effective on the wisher's own emotions. She would wish away the feelings she had for Rhys Lucifer. She would wish to forget the rotten toad had ever existed. She would wish—

Remi went still as a key slid into the front door's lock. The latch turned and she stared with wide, teary eyes as Rhys strolled into the penthouse, followed by Quin and Thorne. Rhys' eyes met hers, the smile on his face falling as he saw the stricken look on hers. He rushed forward.

"Remi, what's wrong..." His words trailed off as he noticed she was looking at his computer. All the color drained from his face. "Love, I can explain."

Remi wiped her eyes and stood. She didn't say a word to him, just stepped around the coffee table.

"What's going on?" Thorne asked, though it sounded distant. He and Quin moved to stand near the stairs.

Remi didn't answer them. Rhys, looking desperate, stretched out his hand to her. "Remi, it's not what you think—"

"Don't touch me!" she screamed. Something in her snapped, the powers she'd worked so hard to keep leashed exploding from her body. All three Lucifers went flying through the air while the furniture slid across the floor. Rhys slammed into the wall near the mounted TV.

His face was twisted with pain as her powers held him in place. The glamour chain around her neck shattered, and she knew without looking in a mirror that her irises were burning red. "You used me," she cried, her voice breaking with pain. Despite her rage, the tears continued to flow.

Rhys lifted his eyes to her. "I…didn't," he gritted. "I swear I didn't know —"

"*Liar!*" The TV cracked, as did the windows and glass leading to the terrace. "Stay the hell away from me. I never want to see you again."

Releasing her powers, she stomped toward the front door. Rhys, Quin and Thorne all dropped like flies to the floor. Rhys stood to his feet, still trying to approach her. "Remi, please, I didn't —"

Without looking, she threw her hand up. Rhys went flying across the living room to slam into the glass sliding door. Having already been cracked, it shattered upon impact. It wouldn't kill or cause any serious damage, as demons were swift healers, but it still had to hurt like a bitch.

Remi snatched the front door open, almost ripping off the latch. Without a backward glance, she left everything behind — Rhys, his brothers, her belongings…everything. The life she'd worked so hard to build and maintain and the secret she'd gone above and beyond to protect were now ruined. Everything had come crashing down.

However, none of that could hold a candle to the pain in her heart — the cold, dark feeling of something spreading through her body until she was completely numb.

It was the pain of betrayal.

"What the fuck just happened?" Thorne exclaimed. With his hands, he checked over his chest and face for some sign of injury.

Rhys groaned, shaking shards of glass from his hair. He stood, pain rippling through him. Not only was he covered in deep scratches from broken glass, he was sure he had at least one cracked rib. It was nothing that wouldn't heal in an hour or two, but it still fucking hurt.

"Rhys, what the hell was that?" Thorne demanded, ambling onto the patio. When he reached out a helping hand, Rhys swiped it away.

"*That*," Quin announced, "was the power of an angry deity."

"What?" Thorne approached the coffee table, where Quin turned the laptop toward both of them.

Rhys clenched his teeth and stepped over the threshold. He steadied himself on the back of the couch. "Damn," he gritted. When his vision cleared, he peered around the room. "Remi?"

"She's gone, man," Quin muttered.

Alarmed, Rhys straightened. The aches lingered through his body, but it was forgotten as he limped toward the front door. He scowled when Quin blocked his path, refusing to let him leave. "What the hell are you doing? Get out of my way."

Quin crossed his arms, his brows snapping together. "Do you want a repeat of what just happened? She'll send you flying toward the Atlantic next."

"I don't care. I need to talk to her."

"Why?" His brother's eyes hardened. "So you can fool her into believing you actually give a damn about anything more than her background?"

Rhys curled his lips into a snarl. He grabbed Quin by the collar of his shirt, unconcerned that his younger brother had a good few inches on him. They all knew that if they went head-to-head in a brawl, Rhys had the upper hand because he was the eldest. He'd gained superior powers to his brothers. "I don't give two shits about her background, and I need to make sure she knows that."

Quin shoved Rhys away from him, his expression the same. "It's funny how you had a change of heart overnight. You, the one who keeps everyone at arm's length so they don't get attached to you. Yet after finding out who she was, you desire a relationship with her."

"Fuck you," Rhys spat. "Remi could be from Troll Valley for all I care."

"Then why did you feel the need to do a background search on her?"

"That was before I realized I was in love with her!" Rhys paced, shoving his hands through his hair. The need to get to Remi and fix this misunderstanding was driving him insane. "I wanted to know how she was able to perform Ivan's job so easily, so I had Kelle do a brief search on her, only to find out that Remington Sawyer doesn't exist in Elysium. Of course, that only made me more curious, so I hired a PI, but I realized nothing he found would even matter. I love her as she is. She makes me…feel."

A muscle in Quin's jaw ticked. "Feel what?"

Rhys sighed, staring off into the night sky beyond the broken glass door. His voice turned quiet.

"Everything. I feel complete with her. She makes me laugh until my sides hurt. She isn't afraid to say what's on her mind to anyone. She's not afraid of me, nor does she see me as Elysium's next ruler. She doesn't care for my name or my money. It's like she sees through all of that, like she sees right through *me*. With her, I'm not Rhys Lucifer, co-owner of EUC, first-born son of Damien Lucifer. I'm not her boss. I'm just…Rhys, an average man. She eases the burdens I have to deal with. And her smile—"

"Holy fuck, dude. We get it," Thorne cut in, glaring. "You just went sappy as hell on us."

Rhys blinked. The words had spilled from his mouth so easily, verbal renditions of his inner thoughts. He only wished he'd had the sense to tell Remi of his feelings sooner. He'd wanted to wait until he had her alone in the perfect setting—under the moonlight, while they walked along the beach, hand-in-hand. Then, after he'd built up the courage, he was going to turn to her and confess everything he felt for her. He was going to tell her how much he cared about her, how he wanted them to go far beyond having a physical relationship, how the mark he'd left on her neck was proof of his feelings.

And yet, he'd waited too long. Remi thought he'd been using her, that after finding out about how valuable she was, he only wanted her for political gain. God below, he was a fucking idiot. He should have recognized his feelings sooner, should have courted her properly and not run away from his emotions.

With a sharp shake of his head, he tried once again to step around Quin. Instead of blocking him, his brother grabbed him by the forearm with a firm grip.

Rhys glared at him, prepared to bark an expletive, but Quin shook his head.

"You can't go after her right now," he said. "Her powers—"

"She can throw me however many times she'd like. I don't care. I need to get to her."

"No, you need to stay here and give her some space." That was from Thorne, who was still sitting in front of Rhys' laptop. "It's not just about you, man. She's hurt, and if you approach her, you'll not only risk her lashing out at you again, but also anyone else around her. This entire resort is crawling with humans. You might be able to take another blast of her powers, but I assure you they can't. Mortals are so…fragile."

Rhys wanted to argue against his brother's logic, but no words would form. Though he wasn't fond of humans, the voice in the back of his mind warned that Remi could kill dozens of them at once if she lashed out. The resulting chaos would not only affect the mundane activities on the resort, but the sudden rush would set EUC back a couple of weeks, both his division and his brothers'.

Plus, he knew Remi well enough to know that if she killed innocents by accident, she'd never forgive herself.

He forced himself to relax, though tension still kept his shoulders tight. "So, what? We just let her walk around all by herself? What if she doesn't return? And gods forbid, what if one of the other families happen across her and learn who and what she is? She isn't supposed to have any powers topside."

Quin released him and took a step back. He reached into the pocket of his khakis and pulled out a travel-sized bottle of sanitizer. He squirted a large dollop into his hand and put it to work. "She won't be alone. I'll have Maya and Carmen find her and stay close. Women need each other's companionship in times like these, and those three have become close this past week."

Rhys nodded, though he still wanted to go himself. He wanted to find Remi and kiss away those sorrowful eyes she'd shot him. He wanted to make this right. The sooner the better. However, he was wise enough to know that his brothers were correct. This was one issue he couldn't resolve alone.

Sighing, he crossed to the kitchen to pour himself a shot of brandy. When that wasn't good enough, he tossed aside the glass and took a long swig straight from the bottle. The burn in his throat began to soothe the fear in his heart, though his worry over Remi's wellbeing remained.

He carried the bottle toward the living room and flopped down on one of the disorderly couches. A sudden thought occurred, and he turned to Quin with narrowed eyes. His brother pulled his phone away from his ear, presumably having spoken to Maya or Carmen. "How come you didn't bat an eye over finding out about her powers? Even Thorne was surprised, but it seemed like you already knew."

Quin shrugged without a shred of apology. "That's because I did. She told me yesterday."

"What?"

Quin scrolled through his phone, unconcerned with Rhys' shock. "Yeah, she was upset because she thought you were mad at her for eating breakfast with Graham, so I got her to open up."

"Wait—*what*?"

"She let it slip that she was born topside. From then, she told me she was half-djinni, half-shaman. After that, it took about five seconds to piece the puzzle together."

"No, back up a pace," Rhys growled, dozens of questions running through his mind at once. "She ate breakfast with Graham? A Belial? What the devil was she thinking? And how come you didn't tell me she was—"

Quin counted off his fingers. "One, I don't work for you. Two, you aren't my ruler yet. Three, I was sworn to secrecy. Four, I don't answer to you. Five, you were being a dick and ignoring her for two days because you were too much of a pussy to admit you had feelings for her. I can spend all night giving you reasons, brother. Believe me when I say the list is endless."

Rhys grunted, but he didn't say anything further. He just took another long swig of the brandy while Thorne chuckled. Rhys shot him a glare next. "Did you know about any of this?"

Thorne snorted. "No, but if I had, I wouldn't have told you regardless."

"*Et tu*, asshole?"

"Asshole I may be, but I'm not the one at risk of losing the best thing to ever happen to me, now am I?"

The words were meant to be cruel—and they were. It was a slap in the face because they all knew it was true. Remi really was the best thing to enter his life. From the first day he'd caught sight of her, his world had changed. *He* had changed, for the better.

And because of his poor decision-making, he was about to lose it all in just one night.

Chapter Sixteen

Remi didn't know how much time had passed since she'd stormed out of the penthouse, but by the time she came to a stop, she was on the beach with the Fontainebleau no longer visible in the distance. She hadn't grabbed any shoes before leaving, so walking barefoot along the streets of Miami Beach had torn her stockings. Rocks and broken glass had cut deep into her skin, though she hadn't noticed until the adrenaline had died down. Her feet were aching and she longed for a hot shower, but she'd be damned if she was going anywhere near Rhys again.

The anger had burned away and she'd cried all the tears her body could produce in one night, so all she could do was wallow in her own misery. She sat on a bench at the end of a wooden pier that stretched a quarter of a mile past the sand, listening to the waves crashing against the pillars. It was comforting, reminding her of the time her family had visited one of their vacation homes in California. She and Jericho would always sneak off in the middle of the night to sit on the beach and watch the waves. Though their personalities were different, they had been the best of friends.

Remi sighed, wishing she could reach out to her younger sister. She craved to feel her companionship again, to have someone who *actually* knew her comfort her during the most painful time of her life.

Maya and Carmen had approached her hours before, but Remi had declined their company and asked them to leave her be. They'd refused, of course, saying something about being concerned for her. After a while, they'd walked with neither saying a word. Just plain silence. She'd known they were both exhausted, but they'd stayed by her side, and she'd been touched by their worry for her. Still, she'd made a small promise to return to the hotel sooner or later. She'd taken Maya's offer to stay in her room instead of the penthouse.

Remi glanced at her watch, but her powers from earlier had cracked the screen and destroyed the battery that powered it. She sighed, tilting her head back to look up at the crescent of the moon high in the sky. If she had to guess, she'd say it was somewhere after midnight. She didn't have her phone, nor had she grabbed her purse containing her wallet. That meant no money for a cab, and it was a pretty long walk back to the hotel.

She bit the inside of her cheek when she tried to put pressure on her bleeding feet to stand, a small sob escaping as she fell back to the bench. Her eyes stung and she punched the wood in frustration.

Great. Not only did she have her first broken heart, but she was miles away from the hotel and couldn't even stand. She would need a pair of tweezers to dig the shards of glass out of her skin, but so long as they remained in place, her feet weren't going to heal anytime soon.

She brought her palms up to cover her eyes, her shoulders shaking, though she still didn't cry. She couldn't. She was just bone-weary, and the more the night dragged on, the worse it got.

Why did she have to do something stupid like falling in love with a devil? A manipulative jackass of a devil who'd used her, made her believe he gave a damn about anyone but himself. For a moment she'd actually thought —

She gave a bitter laugh. She'd thought what? That he cared about her and wanted a real relationship? That he'd declare his undying love for her, get down on one silk-clad knee, and ask her to be his mate for the rest of eternity? Yeah, bullshit. Rhys had played his part well. She'd known he wanted to seduce her into becoming his COO, but it was so much more than that. Now that he knew who and what she was, he thought he could trick her into falling in love with him using his sweet words and caresses.

The memories of their night together brought on a fresh wave of pain. Her eyes pricked with tears. Damn, she'd thought she cried them all out, but apparently not. His stupid plan had worked in the end. Somewhere along the way she'd fallen in love with him. He must have seen it with his devil powers and jumped at the first opportunity.

Gods, she was an idiot. Maybe her parents had been right. True love and friendship would never exist for her. People would try to use her for their own selfishness. That was why it would have been better if they'd paired her up instead of her looking for her own man. She hadn't believed it at first, but tonight had been a gigantic slap in the face. Her parents had forewarned her of this very thing happening. Hell, their own marriage was a sham. Despite how lovey-dovey they pretended to be for the public, none of it was real. It was nothing more than a loveless joining of a power couple who'd combined forces to benefit themselves — her father so he could become filthy rich and her mother so she could remain in the mortal world.

Remi covered her face and sighed. Was that all the world had to offer? Was that all she had to look forward to in life? Playing the docile trophy wife to a man who would never love her for *her*? It wouldn't have been so bad if she could have run the family company herself, or at the very least have had some small say in it, but she hadn't even been allowed to do that. Her mother had embraced her lifestyle, welcomed it because she didn't care for the emotions of the heart. Even Jericho had expressed a desire to live like that, never having to lift a finger to work, spending everyday shopping and catering to herself while her hubby did everything else. All she'd have to do was stand at his side when necessary and provide him with an heir.

She, however, was different. She didn't want any of that. If she were to take a husband, she wanted it to be out of love. If she were to bear children, it would be out of love. If she were to stand at a powerful man's side while he ran a multi-million-dollar company that required her support and care, it would be out of love.

Not for politics or riches or namesake. She wanted to love and be loved for *who* she was, not *what* she was. And she'd thought maybe she'd found it. When she'd peeked inside Rhys' heart and seen that he wanted her on more than a physical level, she'd thought he was the one.

But it had all been a stupid, ridiculous lie. She'd read him incorrectly — or he was able to alter his feelings to make her see something that wasn't there. He was a devil, after all. They could see and manipulate everyone else's feelings, so why wouldn't they be able to do the same to their own?

"Don't you know it's dangerous for a woman to be out at night all alone?" a voice smooth enough to melt butter called out.

Remi stiffened, glancing up to peer at Graham's tall form approaching her. She was too far from the shore and lights for anyone to make out her form. "What are you doing here?" she questioned, not bothering to hide her suspicion.

Maya and Carmen had left her alone hours ago, so they didn't know where she was. If anything, she'd expected to see one of the Lucifers, not Graham.

He tilted his head and gave a small smile, stopping a few feet in front of her. "Would you believe I was merely taking a walk to view the water and happened upon you?"

"This far from the hotel, when there are a half-dozen other piers between here and there? Not even a little bit."

He chuckled and shook his head. He sat on the opposite end of the bench Remi was on — far enough away to where there was a good four feet of space between them, yet way too close for her liking.

"I'd heard there was a fight in the Sorrento Penthouse that caused plenty of broken glass. The humans called the police out of concern, which, of course, has the entire hotel buzzing with activity. Then one of my cousins spotted you exiting the hotel with tears in your eyes. I grew worried."

Remi wiped her face with the back of her hand, turning to him. His story seemed plausible and she didn't detect any lies, but she couldn't shake the feeling that something was off about him being there. "*You* were worried," she repeated slowly. "You don't even know me."

He lifted a brow. "I've spoken with you plenty of times this past week to learn enough to pique my interest. You are a fascinating woman, Remi."

She resisted the urge to roll her eyes. Was he hitting on her with bloody feet, a tear-streaked face, runny nose and swollen eyes? Plus, with all the walking she'd done, she was sure she smelled like the very ass of hell. "So, out of the kindness of your heart, you decided to come check up on me? How did you even find me?"

It was dark where they were, and it happened so fast that Remi could have imagined it, but she didn't think she had. There was a tick in his jaw, a small sign that her words had annoyed him. She opened her powers to peer into his heart, frowning when she saw the same desperation lurking as it had the first time she'd met him, only it was more profound. It was the type of desperation she'd seen push people to do vile things to get what they wanted.

And Remi was positive she had whatever Graham Belial wanted. She just wasn't sure what it was yet.

His charming smile returned, a mask of playful handsomeness covering whatever true intentions lay beneath. "Being topside may weaken our powers, Remi, but upirs still have stronger senses. I followed your scent until I caught up with you."

Remi shifted in her seat, subtly inching away from him until her ass was almost hanging off the end. "Well, thanks for your concern, but I'm fine. I just wanted to get some fresh air for a while."

He glanced at her feet, his nose twitching as if scenting her blood. "I'll give you a ride back. Your feet are injured."

She waved that aside. "It's nothing, just a shallow cut. It's probably already healed by now." That was a lie, but she hoped he wouldn't catch on to it. "Go ahead without me."

That muscle ticked in his jaw again and Remi caught the twitch of his lips as if he wanted to growl at her. He instead flashed her a tight smile, one that was forced. He slid half the distance near her, turning to face her. "I can't leave you out here all alone, especially when you can't even walk. Come. Let me take care of you." He leaned forward to peer into her eyes.

His tiny pupils expanded to swallow all traces of blue. His voice dropped to a low, seductive pitch, one that was used to entrance people to get them to do his bidding. For a moment, Remi swayed toward him as she fought to keep from falling under his enchantment. "I can treat you far better than Rhys ever could. I'll treat you like the queen you are, Remi. Together we can rule all of Sheol."

And there it was, the reason for his choking desperation, the reason he'd spent hours following her trail, waiting until she was alone and vulnerable to try to bend her will. He knew what she was, and like everyone else, he wanted to use her.

Her muscles clenched as her fight-or-flight instincts kicked into high gear. While her mind was running rampant, she couldn't move, not even an inch.

Graham's upir powers gave him control, his hypnotizing gaze boring into her until all she could do was watch him lean closer to her. Remi tried to fight his control over her, but his powers were far too strong in her weak state.

She couldn't even blink. He held her gaze, a triumphant smile curling his lips as his sour desperation reached his peak. "At last, you're mine," he growled. He pulled his lips back and Remi watched in horror as his fangs lengthened to long razors, the needlepoint tips heading straight for her neck.

He was going to bite her. He was going to leave his mark and claim her, and there wasn't a damn thing she could do about it. A tear rolled down her cheek and she mentally called out for anyone to come by and save her. *No, not just anyone.* She wanted Rhys. Despite the pain and anger he'd caused, at least he'd never taken control over her and tried to force himself on her. Everything she'd done with Rhys had been given freely.

More tears fell and fear settled in her gut when Graham gripped her chin in a painful vise, tilting her head to bare her neck. Her heart raced, seeming to pound inside her head. Inside, she screamed, begging to be let free. Outside, all she could do was watch.

Graham tensed all of a sudden. He yanked the collar of her shirt aside, sucking in a sharp breath. It was the area that had been sore all day, but she hadn't taken a look at it. She'd been running late for the meeting after falling asleep in her bath, so had thrown on her clothes and taken off. Then, the other events of the day had taken her mind off it.

"That son of a bitch," Graham snarled, pushing away from her. Remi fell to the ground, her body jarring against the wooden panels that made up the dock. Her chin connected with one of the boards, making her cry out in pain. Free from the enchantment, she rolled onto her back, doing her best to scoot away from Graham.

His face was twisted with fury. He no longer tried to hide behind that playful mask he always wore. She could almost feel the rage rolling off him. "You allowed that bastard to claim you first?"

"W-what?" she choked out.

He took a step toward Remi. Her eyes flew wide. She continued scrambling backward until her back pressed into the railing of the pier. Graham closed in on her, his lips curled to reveal fangs long and wicked enough to tear her throat out. He shot his hand out to pinch where her shoulder and neck met, the spot where Rhys had bitten into her as he'd climaxed the previous night. She cried at the pressure he put on the tender area.

"You are carrying Rhys' mark," he growled, his eyes burning into her. "That bastard got to you before I could."

He gripped her by the throat, squeezing until she could no longer breathe. She clawed at his wrist, but all it made him do was squeeze harder. "No matter," he said, moving his nose until it was an inch from hers. "I'll just have to keep you hidden until the next full moon before claiming you."

Remi squeezed her eyes shut, desperate to gulp in a breath of air. "Why?" she wheezed. Her eyes stung and darkness was creeping along the edge of her vision.

He snorted. "It's simple, really." He loosened his hold just enough for her to gasp in air. "At first I sought to steal you from him. That pathetic worm couldn't tear his eyes away from you for one moment this past week. It would have pleased me greatly to see the look on his face when he discovered that you had your sights on someone else—me." He chuckled, amusement taking over the anger. "Then I discovered who and what you really are."

His eyes twinkled with a sickening pleasure as they once again met hers. "Hades' own granddaughter. Do you know how valuable it would be to mate a direct descendant of a god? How powerful our children will be? Watching Rhys lose the woman he loves to his greatest nemesis is just the cherry on top. Gods, it would have been the perfect plan." His anger returned and he once again tightened his hold on her neck, glaring at her. "That is until he marked you. That puts a damper on my plans—but no worries. I'll have to chain you down until his mark fades before making you mine."

Hatred blossomed in Remi's heart over his words— those sick, horrifying words. How could anyone, demon or not, think to do something so cruel and be fine with it? Remi's gut clenched and bile rose in her throat. She tried calling on her powers, but the lack of oxygen made it impossible for her to concentrate enough.

She swung her fists wildly, hoping to land a blow to his face—anything to get him to release his hold for just a few seconds. When her fist connected with his jaw, he let out an angry grunt and shook her hard enough that she bit her own tongue. "You bitch! I'll—"

In the distance, someone let out a loud, angry roar— a roar that didn't sound remotely human. Graham froze, and in the next instant, he was flung from her. His back slammed into the railing on the other side of the pier's end. Remi fell forward, coughing and trying to gulp in large breaths of air.

She looked up to see Rhys and Graham going at it like wild dogs. Fists connected with jaws, growls erupted and Remi heard the sickening crunch of bone from one of them. She'd seen fights before, fights between humans and fights between demons. However, she'd never seen one so violent. Years of hostile feelings were embedded in every punch each man threw, and Remi could see why the Séance Convention was only held topside. The two looked like they were trying to kill each other.

Remi felt she should step in and do something, but she'd be damned if she got caught up in the middle of those two. Her powers were weak, along with the rest of her, so even if she could use them, she wouldn't have much control. She could risk hurting Rhys in the process.

"Remi!"

She jerked her head to the side, her eyes tearing when Quin approached her, blood trailing from a broken nose. She gasped. "Your face…"

He shrugged, crouching before her. "You should be more concerned with yourself. Are you all right?"

She shook her head, returning her wide eyes to see Rhys knock Graham to the ground. In a split second, he was on top of the upir, beating the shit of him. One particularly strong punch sent Graham's body weak, his eyes rolling into the back of his head, yet Rhys continued to pummel him. Quin walked over to place a hand on his brother's shoulder, but Rhys shrugged him off and continued to beat into Graham's face.

"Rhys, stop," Remi pleaded. "It's over."

To her surprise, he halted mid-punch. He hovered his fist a foot away from Graham's face, which was dripping with blood, though she wasn't sure if it belonged to him or the man under him. He shook as if he could barely control the urge to not continue his assault.

With a loud growl, he shoved away from his unconscious opponent and stalked toward her, a thunderous look on his face. His glamour necklace must have broken in the melee, because his eyes were blazing red and his horns were standing tall and proud. Remi swallowed hard, having never seen him so angry. He looked every bit like the devil he was. It was quite terrifying.

Yet she wasn't afraid of him. She was afraid of what would have happened had he not shown up in time. Tears filled her eyes once more, though she couldn't say what she was crying for — pain over Rhys' betrayal of her, the pain pounding through more than one limb on her body, the fear that Graham had been about five seconds away from rendering her unconscious and doing the-gods-know-what to her, relief at seeing Rhys despite the sadness she still felt.

She didn't know which was the case — or if perhaps it was a combination of everything. What she did know was that she'd been saved by the devil she'd fallen in love with.

In a gesture far more tender than she would have thought him capable of in his fury, Rhys scooped her into his arms, cradling her shivering body to his chest. "I'm so sorry, Remi," he whispered, his hoarse voice filled with just as much emotion as she felt. "Let's go home."

Remi could only nod and lean into him. Her eyes drifted closed as a warmth only Rhys could provide filled the aching hole in her chest. How was it that a man so cold and callous could make her feel that way?

Even after he'd betrayed her, he was still the one thing she wanted — no, *needed* — to feel at peace. It was odd — odd and terrifying and beautiful in the strangest way.

It was too bad it wouldn't last. The night's events had made it clear that people couldn't be trusted with her secret. There was no place for her anywhere — not topside, not in Sheol, not even at home with her parents.

I don't belong anywhere.

Chapter Seventeen

Rhys tugged the door to Remi's new bedroom closed, rubbing a hand through his hair in frustration. He pulled his hand away, wincing at the sight of his busted knuckles. The cuts on them had already healed overnight, but the purple bruises were deep. They wouldn't disappear until the next day or the day after, at the latest.

He squeezed both hands closed and a fresh wave of anger washed over him. He imagined it was Graham's cowardly neck in his hands.

For hours, Maya and Carmen had followed Remi, and when she'd asked them to return to the hotel, they'd only fallen back and tailed her, keeping out of sight. The ladies had kept Quin updated every hour. Even if Quin had told them to return, they would have refused unless Remi was ready to come with them. Rhys had been grateful for them, pleased that Remi hadn't been alone.

Well, pleased up until Maya called and said the Belials had driven past Remi more than once. After that, Rhys couldn't contain himself. He and his brothers had shot out of the room, stuffed themselves into a rental car and hightailed it down to the beach. The ladies had been ordered to keep watch but not get involved with the Belials. Though they were both tough, they weren't skilled at fighting. Maya was unable to shift, and Carmen couldn't use her powers topside, so they wouldn't have been much help, even if they'd wanted to.

When Rhys and his brothers had made it to the pier Remi was on, Graham's two cousins had shuffled out of their limo and attacked them, having been ordered not to let anyone get close. Quin and Thorne had fought the bastards off while Rhys had taken off toward Graham.

As he'd neared, all he'd seen before his vision went red was his enemy squeezing the life out of Remi. He couldn't recall much of what had happened after that. It had all been a blur. The only thing in his mind had been the primal need to destroy whoever had sought to harm his woman.

The next thing he'd known, he'd been in the back seat of the rental car with Remi curled in his arms. No one had spoken for the entire ride. His brothers, Maya and Carmen had all known that if they had been just a few seconds too late, Remi would have been lost to them forever. The thought had been so bloody unbearable that he'd held her tighter than had been necessary.

Rhys flinched when a hand touched his shoulder, his body still in battle mode, despite his having returned to his suite, showered and dressed in pajama pants. He peered into Thorne's eyes that were so much like his own. "You good, man?" his brother asked. It was one of those rare times when he was showing genuine concern, for both Rhys and Remi.

Rhys huffed. "As good as I can be right now." He clenched his hands and jaw. "I still want to go back and strangle that bastard for touching Remi."

Thorne nodded, shoving his hands in his pockets. He had a cut across the curve of his cheekbone and a healing bruise at his temple. "I feel you, brother." He quirked his lips into a half-smile. "But you beat the living shit out of him. Seriously… I didn't even know you could get that mad."

Rhys snorted with humor, moving away from the door and toward the living room. They'd been placed in a new suite, thanks to Remi's powers destroying most of the Sorrento Penthouse. While the hotel managers had been livid at the destruction, Rhys had assured them he would pay out of pocket for the damages. The new place was just as luxurious, though smaller and on just one floor. It was a two-bedroom and his brothers and their workers had helped to transfer his and Remi's belongings to their new room.

With a sigh, he sat on the edge of the couch. Quin and Thorne were sitting around him. Maya and Carmen were sleeping in from having stayed up so late. Rhys had emailed Kelle to get the two women gifts to thank them for their loyalty and protection of Remi. Because they would have done so even if Quin hadn't asked, he wanted to thank them personally.

Colin, Desmond and Bobby had all been caught up on last night's events — minus the bit about Remi being part-deity, of course. That was a secret of hers he didn't want anyone to know unless she told them. He peered at the closed door she slept behind.

It was just a bit past noon, and he was thankful they didn't have to meet until later for the banquet. Hell, at that point he wanted to forgo the dinner altogether and just stay in bed with Remi, simply holding her. He couldn't give two shits about the convention, or policies or anything of the sort. None of that mattered.

"She's going to be okay," Quin said, causing Rhys' attention to turn to him. His broken nose had already healed, as had the small cut that had split his lower lip. "She needs all the rest she can get after last night."

"I know," he breathed, leaning back on the cushion of the couch. "I just… I keep thinking about what would have happened if the ladies hadn't followed her — or if we'd made it to her too late. It pisses me off that I couldn't protect her."

"But you did. She's here with us now. She's safe."

"That's not what I mean." He scrubbed his hands over his face, closing his eyes while he spoke to his brothers. "I only got Kelle to do a background on Remi out of curiosity. I wanted to know more about this mysterious woman who seemed far too perfect to do the toughest job in my division. Before I knew it, I was already mad for her. I realized it didn't matter to me who she was, where she came from or what runs through her blood. She's perfect, just the way she is."

"Here we go with the sappy shit again," Thorne groaned in dismay.

Rhys threw a pillow at him, glaring. "I mean it. One day you'll be in the same boat I'm in, and I'm going to laugh my ass off."

Thorne rolled his eyes. "Doubtful, brother. This stallion isn't meant to be tamed."

Quin snorted, leaning back in the armchair he sat in. "Go on, Rhys."

Rhys looked past him toward the balcony. The sun was shining bright on the blue-green ocean, causing the water to sparkle like it was adorned with diamonds. "Even when Kelle sent me those emails, I was shocked, but I had no desire to ask Remi or mention it to her. I wanted her secret protected at all costs. I wanted her to be able to tell me on her own, so I was prepared to keep my mouth shut for however long I needed to. I wanted her to know she could trust me."

He shook his head. "I can only imagine how hard it must have been for her to spend all this time guarding her secret, unable to get close to anyone for fear they would do exactly what Graham attempted. She must have been so…lonely. I keep to myself too, but at least I have you bastards to lean on if I need it. You two know damn near everything about me. Who does she have?"

He sank farther into his seat, folding his arms behind his head as he continued to gaze out of the sliding glass doors. He felt like he was in a damn therapy session, voicing all his thoughts and feelings to his brothers. He'd never done so before, never felt the need to be so open. But something had changed in him this past week. Spending time with Remi had allowed him to see that he had people around him who cared about him, who he could share himself with. It was thanks to her that the wall that had separated him from all others, including his brothers, had fallen.

Oh, he damn sure wasn't ready to go out and shout his feelings to the world, but this was a start. He didn't feel so alone anymore, not since he'd met Remi. And now he was facing the possibility of losing her.

While she'd clung to him last night, he had no delusions that she'd forgiven him. She could very well walk out of the door the moment she woke up and never looked back.

"Why did you claim her?" Quin asked. "Was it because you wanted to use her for your selfishness, as Graham did? Or because you need a mate before your hundredth birthday?"

Thorne sat up straighter in his seat, but Rhys remained as he was. He scowled. "You know damn well neither of those was the case, not with her. Remi is the first woman… No. She's the first *person* I've ever felt connected to like this. She gives me hope and happiness. As corny as it sounds, she makes me want to be a better demon."

"Yeah, corny as hell," Thorne grumbled. "I'm getting a fucking cavity from all this sweet talk."

This time Quin threw something at his head. "Shut it. Continue, Rhys."

"I want to do everything I can to please her and make her happy. I want her to know I'll sacrifice everything to make sure she never sheds another tear. I claimed her by accident, but in no way was it a mistake. There's no denying I want her as my mate, not because of her blood, or her parents, or grandparents or any of that shit. When I look at her, I see Remi—not a wish granter, not a topsider, not a deity. She's just Remi, the extraordinary data clerk who stole my breath away from the very first day. I love her exactly the way she is. I just hope with everything in me that she'll give me the opportunity to prove it to her."

"I will," a voice said softly.

Rhys shot up like a rocket, his eyes going wide when he saw Remi standing in the doorway separating the living room from the hall. "Remi," he breathed, feeling like he'd been sucker-punched in the gut. "H-how long… How much of that did you hear?"

She gave him a shy smile, rubbing a hand over her bare arm. "All of it." She nodded past him. "Thanks, Quin."

Rhys looked at his brother, who was grinning like the devil he was. "No problem." He and Thorne stood. "We'll give you two some privacy."

As they walked out of the front entrance, heat flooded to Rhys' cheeks at the realization that Quin had urged him to speak his thoughts because Remi had been listening the entire time. He felt played like a fool, but as Remi walked up to him, he made a mental note to thank his brother later.

She moved until she was only a foot away from him. She'd been far too exhausted to move the previous night, so he'd bathed her and dressed her in one of his overlarge T-shirts to provide her with comfort while she slept. The sight of her bare skin had his dick jumping in his pants, but he forced himself to remain calm. Now was not the time to get all excited. He and Remi had so much to talk about.

"Hi," she murmured, fidgeting with the sleeve of the shirt she wore.

"Hi," he breathed. He roamed his eyes over her. Her cuts and bruises had healed, including the purple prints around her neck from Graham's hands. He studied the tender skin, his previous anger returning as the urge to seek the bastard out and kick his ass all over again overcame him. Only this time, he wouldn't stop.

Reading the expression on his face, Remi placed her hands on his cheeks, forcing him to look into her eyes. "I'm fine, okay?" She smoothed her thumbs across his cheekbones. "Everything's healed. I'm a lot tougher than you think."

He placed one of his hands over hers, turning to kiss her palm. "I know that. Gods, you're the strongest woman I know — and I'm not talking about your powers."

Her eyes brimmed with tears, and she lowered her lashes. "I'm sorry about last night."

"Don't be, love." He used a finger to tilt her chin up. "I deserved that. I shouldn't have gone behind your back like I did. I'm sorry. But honestly, I had no intentions on using you or—"

"I know," she whispered. Her fingers tightened on his cheek. "I thought that's all you wanted from me, but not anymore. I can see that now."

He slid his arms around her waist, pressing her close to him. He rested his chin on top of her head. "So, we're good?"

"Yes, Rhys. We're good. But—"

Rhys tensed, pulling away from her. *Oh, gods.* Was she about to deny him? Say she needed space? Were they about to have 'The Talk'? He didn't think he could take any more angst. It was killing him.

"But what?" he asked hesitantly.

"We have to talk about this mark on the side of my neck."

He closed his eyes in dismay. Good gods, it was happening. She was rejecting him. His gut clenched, dread making his throat go dry.

"You don't have one to match."

Rhys stiffened, his eyes flying wide with shock. He looked down at her, saw the wicked gleam in her eyes. He let out a shaky breath. "You mean it?"

She ran her fingers down the side of his cheek to draw little circles on his neck. "I love you, too, Rhys."

Joy exploded inside his chest and a wide grin split his face. He lifted Remi off her feet and spun her around, drawing a breathless laugh from her. When he set her back down, he pressed his lips to hers. She melted against him, letting out a soft sigh.

Rhys pressed his erection against her lower belly, wanting her to feel how hard she made him. She walked him backward, pushing him until he was sitting on the couch, breaking their kiss. He stared up at her, his mouth going dry once more when she pulled his shirt over her head. Next went her lacy black panties.

She was standing before him bare from head-to-toe, and all Rhys could do was gawk. The sun was behind her, providing a soft glow around her body that made her look heaven-sent, like an angel. His breath hitched in his throat and he reached out to cup her hips. "Beautiful," he whispered.

"Tell me something, Rhys," she murmured. He'd broken the chain around his neck in his fight with Graham and hadn't replaced it yet, so his horns were still free. Remi gripped them both from the base, slowly drawing her hands along their length. He shuddered. "Do devils like having their horns played with?"

Rhys' dick damn near exploded, as if she was playing with it instead. For devils, their horns were their biggest erogenous zone. They weren't just for show or status. "You have no fucking idea," he growled, his eyes damn near rolling into his head.

While she stroked his horns, he trailed his fingers over her hips, leaning forward to kiss her stomach. He dipped his tongue inside her belly button, drawing a small hiss from her. He kissed a path downward until he was on his knees before her. Remi watched him with red eyes, and he smiled. She was the sexiest thing he'd ever seen.

Holding her gaze, he tasted her sweetness. She drew in another sharp breath, spreading her legs farther, fully baring herself to him. Rhys hummed in approval, diving in to press his mouth against her. While he lapped at her, she gripped his horns and stroked them with as much expertise as she had his *other* horn.

Still standing, he steadied her with one hand on her hip, the other sliding under her knee to lift it over his shoulder. The new angle allowed him better access to her. He swirled his tongue on her clit, sucking the nub in a way he knew she liked. She paused stroking him, turning instead to grip his hair. "Rhys," she panted, grinding against his mouth in tune with his licks.

Rhys willed his tongue to go faster, sliding along her folds until her thighs and stomach clenched. Suddenly, she pulled away from him, dropping her leg and taking a shaking step back. He tilted his head in confusion.

Her red eyes were lowered, giving him a look that was pure feminine delight. "Sit on the couch."

He did as was told. "Yes, ma'am."

"Slide your pants off," she breathed. "Slowly."

Rhys swallowed, hooking his thumbs in the waistband of his stretchy bottoms, shifting in his seat to lower them off his ass and down his legs. Then he threw them to the side. "Now what?" he husked, enjoying her taking charge. He was always the dominant one with lovers, but having the tables turned on him by Remi was so damn sexy.

"Don't talk," she commanded. She smoothed her hands up her hips and stomach until she was palming both breasts. Rhys swallowed a groan, his mouth parting like a panting dog's. She squeezed, then pressed the full globes together. "Stroke yourself," she whispered. "Pretend like it's between these."

Rhys fisted his shaft, keeping his eyes trained on Remi as she played with her breasts. He timed his strokes with her hands, biting his lower lip to keep from groaning. He wanted to touch her, to have her touch him, but this teasing show was enough to get his blood pumping. His cock was harder than it'd ever been, the tip almost purple in color.

"How does it feel?" she asked.

"Fucking amazing."

"Mm-m." She released herself, flashing him a wicked grin. "Stop touching yourself."

Rhys almost whined at the torture, but his erection jerked when she straddled him, her heat hovering just an inch above him. She placed one hand on his shoulders, the other taking him in a firm hold. She rubbed it through her folds, making them both moan. "I've said it once and I'll say it again," he husked. "You're a dangerous woman."

She pressed her breasts against his chest, kissing the corner of his mouth, then his earlobe. "And don't you forget it," she whispered. Then she impaled herself on his dick.

Rhys threw his head back, gasping as her pussy swallowed him whole. Dear gods, it was the best feeling in the world. He tightened his hold on her waist while she rode him. Like the first time they'd had sex, there was no slow buildup, no dragging it out. Remi rode him as if her life depended on it, and he was right there with her, tilting his hips up to meet her every thrust.

Her breasts were bouncing in his face and he couldn't help himself. He drew one nipple between his lips, sucking the hardened peak while she bounced on his shaft. "Gods, Rhys. I'm so close," she moaned, digging her nails into his shoulders.

Rhys took a moment to pay attention to her other nipple. He was close, too. Just a few more strokes and he was about to explode inside her. Her nipple pulled free with a *pop*, and Rhys tilted his head to the side, baring his neck to her. "You sure you want this?" he managed to grit out.

Please say yes. Please say yes, he begged in his mind. He wanted to complete the mating, to have her permanently carry his mark while he carried hers, so they could live together, overcoming every obstacle and every trial…together…forever.

Instead of giving him an answer, Remi leaned down and bit into his neck hard enough to draw blood. The pain only increased his pleasure. He jerked, giving a loud shout as his orgasm tore through him. At the same time, Remi's core pulsed around him, milking him of every drop of his seed. She cried against him, her body going still while she continued to taste his blood.

She withdrew her teeth and sat back, giving a long sigh of satisfaction. She stared in amazement at her handiwork, while Rhys, in turn, watched his. The bite mark on the crook of her neck and shoulder shifted, morphing into ancient runes that would seal them together. Once completed, the marking looked like a black tribal-style tattoo in the shape of a circle with teeth marks inside.

Pride and joy filled Rhys, as he could now sense everything she felt. Her feelings matched his own. There was no longer any fear. There was no worry, no stress, no sadness, just pure bliss that finally they'd each found something that had eluded them in the past.

Rhys cupped her face in his palms. "Swan," he murmured against her lips.

She lifted a brow. "What?"

"A swan." At her confused look, he smiled. "When I first took you out to dinner at Marino's, you asked me what kind of animal I thought you were, if not a mouse. You remind me of a swan—beautiful, graceful, elegant—yet fierce and bold enough to overcome anything, to conquer any threat. You, my love, are a swan."

She slowly spread her lips into a small, loving smile. She rubbed her hands over his shoulders, up the sides of his neck, then back down. "I love you, Rhys Lucifer."

He kissed her again. "And I love you, Remington Sawyer Lucifer—forever and always."

Chapter Eighteen

It'd been two months since Remi and Rhys had made their mating official, two months filled with so much confusion and so many questions. As expected, the news of their mating had spread like wildfire within the first week, not only across EUC, but across all Elysium. Remi had met Rhys' father, Damien, and while he hadn't been pleased to know his son had mated without informing him, after the first day of meeting Remi, he'd changed his attitude.

Remi had been nervous to meet her new father-in-law, but not afraid—not with Rhys at her side. She'd met the great demon lord with squared shoulders, and it hadn't taken long for her easy wit and charm to enthrall both him and his wife. They'd accepted Remi with warm, open arms. After another two weeks of family dinners and luncheons that they'd invited her to—Rhys, not so much—she'd dropped the bomb on them about who she was. Slowly afterward, the news of Remi's heritage had spread, and while she'd expected everyone to be shocked, not one person she worked with had come to her with a request for her to grant them a wish.

In fact, no one treated her any differently than they had before.

Work had also run with smooth sails. Remi had become Rhys' full-time COO, while also helping him with his workload. It was a lot to do, but they'd made the best of it. Between the two of them, the stress of their work had been kept to a minimum with the bonus that they got to spend every night together.

Well, almost every night. Rhys had been on a business trip to The Meadows and Asphodel for the past week and a half, and she'd only gotten to see him for a few short minutes over video chat. She'd been lonely since then, having to work extra hours to keep herself from pouting all night.

Tonight, however, he was scheduled to fly home. Actually, he was already on the way. It wouldn't take more than thirty minutes, which was perfect timing. Dinner was almost ready, and Remi couldn't wait. She hummed to herself and checked on the chicken in the oven, then straightened. She smoothed her palms over the front of the black silk dress she wore. It was a floor-length gown cut deep to reveal her cleavage with a long slit all the way up one thigh. She'd chosen it for a special occasion, because not only was her mate returning home, but she had some exciting news to share with him.

A knock sounded and she perked up like a puppy. In the distance, Pepper barked and pawed at the door. Remi rushed through her and Rhys' new house toward the front door. Her heart was racing.

With a huge smile, she twisted the knob open. "Hey, sweetie. I wasn't expecting you so — "

Remi trailed off as she stared up at a man who was definitely not her husband. He was way taller and by far the most imposing demon she'd ever encountered — and he was absolutely beautiful. He had perfect alabaster skin without the slightest of blemishes, features so sharp that they could cut diamonds, a nose so straight it could balance a ball and bone-straight black hair, a long river of silk that was almost sweeping the ground. He was dressed in a fancy white toga that was so clean and white that she almost had to shield her eyes from the illumination of it. Hard green eyes that were so bright that it looked like a candle was shining behind them stared down at her quizzically.

She took a step back, frowning. She and Rhys lived at the far end of a private road located on the edge of a quiet suburban neighborhood. Plus, there was a locked iron gate at the end of the driveway that only few people had the code to. There was no way someone had gotten lost. "Um, can I help you?"

The man said nothing, only continued to watch her with that cold, calculating gaze. It wasn't threatening or menacing, but a cold shiver danced down her spine. The man was...unnerving, to say the least. There was a powerful aura radiating from him. It was a cloak of authority that made her want to bow to him.

She gave up her polite smile and settled for an irritated frown when he still said nothing. "Look, buddy. Unless you're selling Pup Scout cookies, I suggest you turn around and head back to wherever you came from."

He looked taken aback, raising a dark brow. Then, he quirked his lips in amusement. It was a tiny movement, one that would have been impossible to notice if not for his close proximity. In silken tones that sent another shiver down her spine, he spoke. It wasn't the delicious shivers of excitement Rhys made her feel. These were… Hell, was there even a word for it? 'Uncomfortable' was a bit of a stretch, but it was damn close.

"You look just like your mother."

Remi paused, her breath freezing in her throat as the blood drained from her face. "You know…my mother?" Well, it shouldn't have been surprising. Everyone knew about her being Elizaroth's daughter by now.

His lips twitched again, this time into a tiny ghost of a smile. "Of course. I raised her, after all."

Remi's eyes flew wide and she studied the man more closely. His eyes gave him away. Only one other person she'd ever met had those same eyes, the almond shapes so much like her own, the color of emeralds under the sunlight. They were almost glowing, which tended to have an intimidating effect on most people.

Her mother had the exact same eyes.

"Hades," she breathed.

This time, he showed teeth when he smiled, teeth that were as white as his toga and so straight that the lines between them were damn near impossible to detect. Only a god could claim such perfection. "My granddaughter. I've longed to meet you."

Remi's heart thundered in her chest. It was a wonder it didn't fly right out of the cavity. "Oh, my gods. This is… I mean, I didn't… I never…"

"Hush, now," he commanded, still smiling. Well, it was his version of a smile. "I blame your mother for keeping you and your sister away from your true heritage."

"You know Jericho?"

His smile faltered, something flashing deep in his eyes. *Sadness, maybe?* It was hard to tell. The god of the underworld was impossible to read. "Jericho," he murmured slowly, testing the name on his tongue. "Remington and Jericho. Interesting names. I have yet to meet her. I only know what my people report back to me. Elizaroth has always been talented at evading my attempts to spy on her."

Remi tilted her head in confusion. "That must be why she always kept us on such a tight leash."

"It would appear so," he agreed. He took in her appearance with a critical eye. "You are going out?"

Heat rose to Remi's cheeks as she felt the ridiculous urge to cover herself. "My mate comes home tonight, in about ten minutes, actually. I haven't seen him in over a week, and I want to tell him—"

She broke off when he lifted another brow at her words.

"Um… Wow, this is embarrassing. I don't even know what to say."

He made a quiet sound, almost like a snort of humor, before taking a step back. "There is no need to say more than what you have, my dear. I am no stranger to the workings of a new mating. I merely wanted to take the opportunity to meet you before returning to Tartarus."

Remi sighed, a twinge of sadness filling her. It was strange. He was a man—her grandfather—whom she'd never met before today, and while most people would feel uncomfortable and terrified with the situation, she just felt…sad. There was so much she wanted to say and ask, and while she'd planned to meet the god somewhere down the line, she hadn't expected it to be like this.

As if reading her mind, Hades gave another tiny 'smile' that she was sure he didn't do often. He waved his hand and two golden coins appeared in his palm. "Pay me a visit soon, Remington. Bring your mate. We have much to discuss. I may be the fearsome god of the underworld, but I do enjoy getting to know my descendants, especially the younger ones like yourself."

Remi took the two coins, a wide smile splitting her face. When she looked up, Hades was already strolling back down the carport. "Hey, does this mean I can call you Pops, or Grandpa or Peepaw?"

Her grandfather stopped midstride, turning a glare over his shoulder that could freeze over the hottest layer of hell. "No. Hades is fine." With that, he disappeared in a cloud of black smoke.

Despite the evil look he'd just given her, Remi chuckled to herself and closed the door. She returned to the kitchen, just as the oven's timer went off. Her entire encounter with Hades had been…odd. Odd, but welcome. She'd be lying if she said she'd always longed to meet the terrifying god of death, but now she had. She looked forward to getting to know him, and best of all, she'd get to drag Rhys down there with her. The god's orders.

Smiling with genuine happiness, she placed the two coins on the island countertop and turned to pull the food out of the oven. It didn't take long before the delicious aroma filled the air. She'd wanted Rhys to come home to a homecooked meal with her wearing an outfit that would have him fighting to decide which he wanted to take a bite out of first.

Her, most likely. They couldn't keep their hands off each other when in the same room.

Just as Remi finished setting everything out, she heard the locks to the front door twist open. Smiling, she picked up her glass of water and leaned back against the kitchen counter, hiding the little giftbox behind her back.

Five seconds later, Rhys turned a corner, his eyes widening at the sight of her. He smiled, tugging at his silk tie. "I see you've been busy, my love."

Remi smiled in return, taking a sip of her glass. "I wanted to surprise you when you came home."

He grinned, closing the distance between them. He nodded at the glass in her hand. "Water, not wine?"

Remi's smile widened. "Water is healthier, don't you think?"

He chuckled. "You look beautiful, Remi." He wrapped his arms around her waist, burying his face in the crook of her neck, placing soft kisses to her mating mark.

"I have so much I want to tell you."

"Mm-m. Can it wait?" He nipped at her skin then licked over it.

"It can, but I don't want to."

He chuckled and pulled back, though he didn't let her go. "Okay, love. Talk to me. How was your week?"

"Lonely," she pouted, "but not terrible. A lot has happened, and you wouldn't believe the latest. But first things first. I have a gift for you." She set her glass down and reached behind her for the long black box draped in velvet. She gave a shy smile, nervousness filling her gut as she handed it to him.

"You didn't have to get me anything," he said. Even so, he opened it. His playful smile vanished, replaced by a look of utter shock. He stared at the opened box for several moments, then her, then back at the box. "Is this…" He swallowed thickly, unshed tears filling his dark eyes. "Is this what I think it is?"

With shaking fingers, he pulled out the pink-and-white plastic stick that had a plus sign on the little screen. He studied it for several more moments.

Remi reached up to frame his face, her own hands shaking. She gave him a reassuring smile. "Yes, Rhys, I'm pregnant. We're going to have a baby."

His breath hitched and he closed his eyes, though Remi could feel his happiness through their mating bond. Rhys dropped to his knees and hugged her waist, planting multiple kisses to her flat stomach. "Thank the gods," he breathed.

Remi laughed, holding his head against her. Her heart was full. Despite the distant pain over missing her sister, she was happy with the life she had—a wonderful, loving mate, a child growing in her belly, a mischievous yet playful puppy, multiple friends who accepted her for who she was and a grandfather who wanted to get to know her.

She'd finally found where she belonged in the world. She had a family again, only this one treated her with love and care.

And she couldn't be any happier.

Guide

Sen and torqs – *forms of demon currency*

Canaan – *the heaven-like realm where mortal gods and angels live*

Topside – *the human world*

Sheol – *the underworld realm that is home to the majority of the demon population. It consists of four regions with different ruling families.*

Elysium – *ruled by Lucifers and home to Elysium Underworld Corporation (EUC)*

Asphodel – *ruled by Dagons and home to Center of Eternal Punishment (CEP)*

The Meadows – *ruled by Levis – Leviathans – and home to Infernal Meadows (IM)*

Abyssia – *ruled by Belials and home to Bell Towers. This is the only region that doesn't house one of the soul collection centers*

Tartarus – *the realm under Sheol where Hades and other high-level gods and demons reside*

Hades – *the god of the underworld who demons see as a prominent political figure. He goes by many names in different religions.*

Want to see more from this author?
Here's a taster for you to enjoy!

The Royal Gordanos:
A Royal's Touch
Makayla Roberts

Excerpt

Humans are such mundane creatures. They carry on with their lives, unaware of just how vast the world truly is.

They're unconscious of the immense number of demons roaming through their cities, living secret lives among them. Demons hide behind magical glamour spells to make themselves invisible to mortal eyes, but many of them just blend in with only the subtlest indications of their natures. Vampires have stunning, heart-wrenching beauty – shifters, the sweltering heat of their skin that is far hotter than a human's and trolls have impenetrably thick skin and a brief flash of red in their eyes when they grow angry.

That was one of the things Ava loved most about humans. They were simple-minded. Where her world was filled with danger, darkness and children of the underworld, humans were oblivious to the mystical existence around them.

She envied that about them. To be able to live their lives with no clue that they were always surrounded by creatures that go bump in the night. It was miraculous how blind they were.

Yes, envious indeed. Yet, at the same time, she couldn't help but admire them.

To have a demon strolling past them every day, even serving the food at a restaurant they frequented — *cough, cough* — yet never even knowing... She only wished to trade places with them. Maybe then she'd be able to get a full night of sleep.

"Don't tell me you're daydreaming again, Ava," a friendly, yet gruff voice called out.

Ava turned a smile on her boss, who was raising a bushy gray eyebrow at her through the small square window separating them. Though he was a rough-looking old man with a perpetual scowl, he had a heart of gold. He'd give the clothes on his back to someone in need.

A trait lacking in the majority of demons.

"Sorry about that, Mr. Tommy," she said. She picked up a thin white rag and tasked herself with wiping down the countertop. The diner she worked in was fairly empty at this time of the morning. The early morning rush had ended, but there were a few customers seated at the tables, finishing off their meals.

Tom's Place wasn't anything special, but there was a certain charm about the diner that made Ava feel comfortable working there. A gray-and-white checkered tile floor complemented baby-blue booths and metal tables. The walls were the same blue, with aged pictures from the diner's first opening in the twenties hanging on the walls. The windows had a faint tint on them to keep the inside cool and shaded, which was perfect for Ava.

She had a mild allergy to the sun's rays.

In all honesty, she didn't need this job. She'd managed to save up a considerable amount of wealth over the years to keep herself comfortable for a while.

However, as a waitress, it was a great way to interact with humans. She enjoyed studying them, learning more about their ways. She'd been sheltered from them until she reached adulthood. When she'd gone off into the world to discover for herself what was out there, she'd developed a substantial fascination with the fragile beings.

It had quickly become her small bit of joy in life — *which is rather…bizarre, isn't it?*

They were a puzzling race. The smallest of incidents could be fatal for them, and they were foolishly driven by their emotions rather than their minds. She didn't understand it in the slightest, but she wanted to. It was intriguing.

But no matter how much she enjoyed watching humans, she couldn't get involved with them any more than that. She'd never forgive herself if anyone was hurt because of her carelessness.

Especially not *that* human. There was one in particular her body craved like no other, which was a very, very dangerous thing in her predicament.

The bell above the diner door rang and the delicious scent of sandalwood filled her nose. *Speak of the devil…* She frowned to herself and looked up at the two men who took a seat at the diner bar, right in front of her. As always.

They were both dressed in uniform and both as handsome as could be. However, it was the one to the right who made her heart skip a beat. The human cop was so good-looking it was almost painful. In all her hundred-plus years of living, she'd seen her share of handsome men. But this one? He took the cake.

He had a crew-cut hairstyle, his hair cut close to his head on the sides, while the remaining dark hair on top was longer and neatly brushed backward. His eyes were a bright golden color, framed by thick, dark lashes that were long enough to make any woman seethe with jealousy. He had a thin, straight nose and a chiseled jawline so sharp that only a master craftsman could have sculpted it with such perfection. And his lips? Full, flawless and made to please a woman.

And when he smiled…

Good gods, when he smiles. His teeth were even and white, his cheeks bearing the deepest set of dimples she'd ever seen. Add to that his six-foot-three muscular build and he was a walking sexual invitation affecting women within a five-mile radius. And Ava was no exception.

Which was what frustrated her more than anything. She couldn't get involved with anyone right now — least of all a human — no matter how much her body ached for his touch.

"Good morning, Aaavaaaa," Marc drawled, those dimples flashing when he grinned.

Ava kept her face blank at the lazy way he drew her name out, but inside her heart was pounding. Even his smooth voice had her shifting her feet as heat began to pool in the pit of her stomach.

She gave him and Duncan a simple nod, ignoring her body's reaction to the sexy male. "Good morning," she responded, avoiding Marc's simmering gaze. "Edith will be over to take your orders shortly."

His dimpled smile never wavered. "Ahh, still too shy to talk to me, are you? It's been how many months now?"

Ava didn't respond as she turned to walk through the door to the kitchen area of the diner.

Too shy to talk to him? Gods. If he knew how bad she wanted him, he'd be running in terror until he reached the Atlantic Ocean.

Shaking the thought from her head, she headed toward the stock room where the other waitress, Edith, was gathering a few items.

She looked over at her. "I was *not* expecting that morning rush today," the aged woman said. "I know it's Friday, but golly."

Ava nodded in agreement. "Right? I have no idea where that crowd even came from. Is there some sort of special event going on in the city?"

Edith's gaze turned thoughtful. "If there is, I haven't heard about it. Chicago is pretty big, so there's no telling."

"Hmm. Well, your favorite customers are here. I'll finish stocking while you take their orders."

Edith blinked in surprise, her wrinkled gaze turning dreamy. "Marc and Duncan?" She let out a little happy squeal, dropping her handful of straws and condiment packets. "Oh, cripes," she muttered, crouching down to pick them up.

Ava got down to help her. "Don't worry about it. I'll get these. You go on."

Edith gave her a small frown. "Ya'know, Ava, I've been wondering for a while now... You're so nice to everyone that comes in but you always avoid those two. Why is that?"

Ava felt her cheeks heat just a bit. *Damn those old eyes of hers.*

She kept her head down, focusing on picking up the dropped items. "No reason," she mumbled. And damn herself for not being a good liar. What was the purpose of being a demon, known for their manipulation and cunning mental prowess, if she couldn't even master the art of telling a lie?

She knew that pathetic excuse wouldn't stop the other woman from prying. She was like a fluttering grandmother, always attempting to piece things together.

"Child, they're both drop-dead gorgeous," the woman continued. "They're cops, and neither of them has a ring on his finger." She paused for a second. "Wait! Could it be *because* they're cops? I know some people who tend to avoid the law at all costs. Is that the reason?" She looked around suspiciously before lowering her voice to a whisper. "Are you on the run from the authorities? Are you worried about getting deported? Don't. I won't rat on you."

Ava let out a small chuckle. In the few months since she'd been working there, she'd learned how much of a chatterbox Edith was. She voiced all her thoughts and opinions without a care in the world. Half the time Ava was sure the woman didn't even realize it. "Deported?" she asked, smiling.

Edith nodded, tapping a bony finger to her wrinkled cheeks in thought. "Yes, deported back to Mexico where you came from."

Ava shook her head. "I'm Italian, Edith, not Mexican. Two completely different countries on two completely different continents."

Edith waved that away. "Whatever. I'm not so good with all these different accents. Too many of them sound alike."

Ava only continued to smile. Despite Edith's claims, Ava's Italian accent was very faint. She'd spent a great number of years all over America, so she often picked up on their ever-changing lingo. The only time it became noticeable was if her emotions surged, which had yet to happen since working here.

"There are plenty of other police officers who come in here, and I have no trouble talking with them," Ava responded. "Honestly, I don't have an issue with either

Duncan or Marc. Let's just say I'm fairly shy around men who look that good." It was a lie, but she couldn't very well tell the woman she didn't talk to Marc because his very presence was enough to make her body tingle with desire. *Talk about embarrassing.*

"Oh well, I suppose that makes sense. Ever since you started working here, you would clam up and act all shy with only those two. Especially Marc. *That's* the one you need to shag."

Ava shook her head again. "Shag? What does that even mean?"

The woman stood up, raised a brow and put a bony hand on her hip. "You know what I mean. He's young and virile. You're young and gorgeous. You're both single. And I see the way you look at each other when no one's looking." She winked at that. "If I was just a few years younger, I'd mount that stallion in a heartbeat."

Ava bit the inside of her cheek to keep from laughing out loud. *A few years younger? Yeah, right.* They both knew full well that Edith was in her seventies — wrinkles, gray hairs and all. "Polite pass, Edith. I'm just not interested in seeing anyone right now."

That much was true, at least. Dating or even purely sexual relationships were impossible for her. *Hell, with my bad luck, it'll probably always be that way.*

"Oh well, your loss then, honey," Edith said, shrugging. She smoothed the front of her apron and straightened her thin shoulders. "How do I look?"

Ava rose as well, smiling warmly. "Fabulous."

Edith grinned and made her way back to the front, putting a little sway in her steps. Ava shook her head, still smiling. *That woman is really something else.* She was living proof that anyone is only as old as they feel. Well, to humans anyway. Time had no meaning to most demons.

She'd grown quite attached to the woman and her husband, Mr. Tommy. Though they had incredibly different personalities, they were both so sweet and generous. There'd been a few times when she'd seen them take people off the streets, offer them a hot meal and warm bed, clean them up and give them a job at the diner before helping them find something better. There weren't very many demons, if any, who would do such a thing without expecting something in return. It was the kind of pure, human love that made them want to help each other.

She placed the fallen items into the trash and washed her hands. She then pulled on a fresh pair of latex gloves, grabbed more condiments and went back to the front, where Edith's flirtatious giggling could be heard.

Ava hid a smile and began stocking the bins underneath the counter a few feet away from them. The woman was married and old enough to have great-grandchildren, yet she still flirted away with the younger men. It was fairly amusing, and the guys all went along with it.

As always, she was aware of Marc's presence. Over the smell of grease, butter and the other employees and customers, his scent stood out the most. It was a mix of his aftershave and his own personal aroma that filled her senses, making her head spin. That alone was enough to drive her mad with want.

And it was such a nuisance. She loved humans, but he stood out like a sore thumb—a very sexy, enticing sore thumb. And it was bloody frustrating because she didn't even know why. Why was it just him she felt so enamored with? Why did she feel such an intense reaction? Why did her heart jump every time her eyes met his? Yes, he was extremely attractive. Then again, so was his partner and several other men she'd come across. *So why only him?*

Speaking of his partner, she looked over at the Scot out of the corner of her eye.

Duncan looked normal enough, but he wasn't human. Oh, he very much smelled like one and did well to hide it, but she knew better. Demons could always sense another demon's presence.

Unlike Marc, Duncan's reddish-brown hair was longer and brushed back, the tips curling around his ears. His face was clean-shaven with a faint scar running from his chin up to his ear. However, it did nothing at all to take away from his handsome features. If anything, it gave him more of a gruff, sexy look, like those proud Highland warriors she'd seen on the covers of romance novels. But there was just something in the air around him that was demonic—a deadly, powerful aura that never failed to make her wary.

Oh, she wasn't afraid of him. She could hold her own against most demons. She did, after all, possess the blood of Royal vampires, some of the strongest demons to ever walk the earth.

However, Duncan was… Hell, she didn't know. His eyes were dark green with flecks of yellow around the pupil, but they held a predatory gleam that hinted at his demon side. It was like he was always searching for his next meal. That made her think he was some sort of shifter. Whether it was canine, feline or something else, she had no idea, but either way, he'd be a dangerous adversary.

Duncan was talking to Edith, making her laugh. When the woman turned away to place their orders, he looked over at Ava out of the corner of his eye, catching her watching him at bay. He winked and gave her a knowing smile. He knew she was a demon as well. It had been evident when they'd first met each other months ago, though neither of them had ever once mentioned it.

And why should they? Most demons were naturally private creatures. It wasn't like they often sat around a campfire holding hands and singing songs about peace and love. The thought made her give a soft snort.

Still… More than once she'd wondered what kind of demon he was and why he was parading around as a human cop. The intelligent look in his eyes told her he was far older than he appeared. He was a demon who'd lived a long life and had many stories to tell.

She gave another small shake of her head. *Oh well.* No need for dwelling on such trivial thoughts. Even if she had the answer to that question, it wouldn't change anything. As much as it would be nice to have demon friends she could feel comfortable around and let her fangs down with once in a while, so to speak, she would just have to keep dreaming. She wasn't the safest person to be around. And Marc…

He was a human. Getting involved with one was something she'd sworn to never do. She'd interact with them, even take their blood when she needed it. But with Marc, she wanted him in a way she hadn't ever felt before.

That in itself was dangerous. She would have to keep her distance from him. She feared that once she gave in to her carnal desires, it would be hard to stop.

And she would never forgive herself if something were to happen to him, all because she'd brought him into her world.

"Hey, Ava, come listen to this story," Edith suddenly called out. "It's intense."

Jarred from her thoughts, Ava bit back a sigh. *Damn you, Edith*, she thought. She was a character, but she was nosey as could be—nosey, and always trying to play matchmaker between her and Marc.

Ava picked up a clean blue towel and slowly walked over to them. The closer she got, the more Marc's scent clouded her mind. He was smirking as if he knew the effect he had on her. *Damn him too.*

Even as she silently cursed him, she was powerless to fight the way her body clenched in response to his look. *I'm worse than a harpy in heat, for crying out loud.*

"Thanks for joining us," he said playfully. Ava shrugged, annoyed that her tongue was dry. The more she looked at him, the more drawn she became. He was undoubtedly human, but he had a certain pull about him that could rival that of a full-grown incubus.

She began to dry the already-dried coffee mugs under the counter, setting them in their proper places as she listened.

Duncan was the one continuing the story. From what she'd learned from Edith, he had been born and raised in Scotland up until he'd been a teenager, then he'd moved to the US where he'd become a full citizen. He still had a thick accent when he spoke.

Although, with him being a demon who probably aged much more slowly than humans, it was no doubt just a cover. Not that he wasn't Scottish... The thick brogue and powerful aura gave him a warrior's presence that couldn't be faked. However, he could have spent several centuries in his homeland before coming here. *Who knows?*

"Anyway, one day we got a call about this drunk guy running down the street in this old neighborhood. It's broad daylight and he's just running, screaming at the top of his lungs. So we answer the call and roll up on this guy, expecting him to be high as shit. When we found him, he was rolling around in a field of grass screaming '*They're inside of me!*' This wasn't the first nut case we'd come across, so the procedure was pretty standard."

While Duncan continued with his story, a prickling sensation slid down Ava's neck, causing her to look up. She glanced around the room, but none of the patrons were out of the ordinary. The feeling became stronger and it was one she was all too familiar with. She narrowed her eyes, peering out of the large, shaded windows. She trusted her senses more than anything, and right now they were telling her something sinister was nearby.

She was never wrong.

Sure enough, across the street in the narrow alley stood a lone, cloaked figure. Even with the daylight outside, it was still dark between the two buildings. The humans on the other side of the street continued walking, completely oblivious to the danger standing within feet of them. To anyone who could see it, it would look like an ordinary person dressed for the changing weather.

To Ava, the figure stood out. It wasn't a human. It was hidden deep in the shadows, but she could make out two glowing-red eyes from under the hood it wore. Even with the distance, her enhanced eyesight allowed her to see the creature open its mouth in a wide grin.

Found you, it mouthed.

Her heart raced in her chest as she broke out in a cold sweat.

Damn, damn, damn. She'd known it might only be a matter of time before she was discovered, but she'd been too reckless. She'd hoped she had finally shaken the ghouls off her tail and had allowed herself to get too comfortable. *Curse it all.*

There was the sound of glass breaking, followed by a sharp pain in her hand, but she didn't even flinch. She glanced down at the shattered cup she'd grasped too tightly, watching as her blood flowed onto the sink and countertop.

She hissed, quickly running the water and holding her hand under the faucet.

By the gods. Now, with the scent of her blood in the air, it'd be even harder to make an escape. She'd just dug her own damn grave.

Edith appeared at her side, trying to help Ava with her wound, even as she was beginning to panic. Even Marc and Duncan look alarmed, and she could see Duncan's nostrils flaring, his eyes widening as he caught her scent.

Shit and double shit.

She had to make a quick escape.

Though most ghouls preferred night over day, there were a few who were strong enough to withstand the burning sunlight for a certain amount of time — like the one across the street, for example. And they were definitely not afraid to kill any humans who came between them and their target. If she stayed much longer, no doubt everyone in the diner would be injured…or worse. They would be collateral damage.

Wrapping her hand in the blue cloth towel, she turned to the small square window separating her from Mr. Tommy. She clutched her bleeding hand to her chest. "Sorry, Mr. Tommy, but I've got to go." She didn't even wait for a response. She took off her apron and sped out of the back, ignoring calls from her coworkers. She burst through the door and raced down the street. She knew the ghoul was following. She could feel it moving swiftly through the streets and alleys, following her scent. Her superior speed was near blinding compared to the ghoul's, but even then she didn't have much time. Once one of those creatures caught a scent, it was damn hard to get rid of them.

She only prayed her sudden departure would cause the creature to avoid harming anyone near the diner.

Home of Erotic Romance

Sign up for our newsletter and find out about all our
romance book releases, eBook sales and promotions,
sneak peeks and FREE romance books!

About the Author

Makayla's love for reading began at the age of twelve when her mother introduced her to the world of mystical creatures. From then on, she discovered a talent for turning her own imagination into words. From fanfictions to short stories to full-length novels and novellas, if she wasn't focused on school activities, she was either reading or writing.

Raised on the coast of Mississippi, Makayla juggles her everyday life between work and being a mom. In her free time, she enjoys binge watching criminal suspense shows, shopping, painting, wood burning, and of course, working on her books.

Makayla enjoys writing stories with strong elements of romance, adventure, and paranormal. Vampires, shifters, fairies, dragons — she loves them all!

Makayla loves to hear from readers. You can find her contact information, website details and author profile page at https://www.totallybound.com